Dillion's Dainty Delight

All the President's Men, Volume 3

Rose Nickol

Published by Rose Nickol, 2021.

DILLION'S DAINTY DELIGHT

First edition. July 6, 2021.

Copyright © 2021 Rose Nickol.

ISBN: 979-8201622749

Written by Rose Nickol.

Also by Rose Nickol

All the President's Men
Derek's Darling Damsel
Dillion's Dainty Delight

Ashcroft Security
Ashcroft Security Saving Lena

Club de Fleur
Club de Fleurs 3: Theresa`
Club de Fleurs 4: Rachel
Club de Fleurs 5: Tina's Twins
Club de Fleurs 2 Sadie
Club de Fleurs Tasha
Club de Fleur Melissa

Club de Fleurs
Club de Fleurs: Jenna

Daddies' Lost Girls
Litte Girl Lost

Heroes of the Heart
Rescuing Their Love Hereos of the Heart Book One
Rescuing Their Love Heroes of the Heart Book Two

Kodiak Matings
Bearly Mated

Standalone
Kodiak Matings Bearly Mated

Watch for more at rosenickol.com.

Table of Contents

Chapter One

Tracy Smith sat on her front stairs waiting for Dillon Polk to pick her up. She had been waiting for several minutes, not because he was late but because she was early. She didn't want him in her house tonight. It wasn't that she didn't trust Dillon but she didn't let anyone in, her house or her life. Tracy kept everything private. She had few friends and liked it that way. She'd been hurt, badly, by someone she trusted and was not going to be in that position again.

Why she had agreed to go to the club with Dillon tonight was beyond her, but she had agreed and, other than being sick, could not get out of it. Part of her knew why she'd consented, because she needed it. BDSM was as much a part of her as her body parts were. She needed the release it gave her, needed the connection to another person she got from it, and no matter what she tried, she couldn't get that release anywhere else. She had tried for years to find something else that would give her that feeling, but nothing did. Her body craved it.

Tracy and Dillon had partnered off and on for two years. He worked with the Secret Service, and she was with the FBI. They had been assigned to the same case several times and worked well together. They also played well together at The Mix, a BDSM club partly owned by Dillon's boss and friend Derek Moore. He introduced Tracy to Dillon one night at the Mix.

Derek was a Dom and knew Tracy's history. When she talked to him about her needs, he promised to introduce her to someone who could help her and not hurt her. He provided a safe place for her to play and watched over her carefully, like an older brother.

The only problem Tracy had with Dillon was that he wanted more than she was willing to give. He wanted to date her, and she just wanted to be friends, play occasionally, and have sex. The sex with Dillon was good, very good. Yep, the friends-with-benefits thing was working very well for her—or had been. Lately, Tracy had started wanting more herself. Maybe it was her internal clock or something, but playing and sex weren't enough. At the end of the night, she still needed something. Her bed was lonely and the house too quiet. She needed something more than Tickles, her cat, to sleep with.

Tracy had fun playing with Dillon at the club, when he wasn't nagging her for more, and they worked great together. He couldn't understand why she wouldn't go out with him anyplace but the club and why she wouldn't let him in her house. The truth was she hadn't wanted him that close at first.

What Tracy never told anybody was that she had been in a D/s relationship for five years before moving to Washington, DC, and becoming an FBI agent. It hadn't ended well. Since then, she never let anyone get close. She figured out by keeping everyone at a distance, she wouldn't get hurt again. Several of her friends had told her she was crazy, and Dillon was the best thing that had ever happened to her, and he was nothing like the man she had been in the relationship with. But, after having her trust broken once, she was not going to let that happen again. She had been in the hospital for days and therapy for months. She played at the club only in front of witnesses. Tonight she was going to change things.

She was starting to feel different about Dillon. She wanted more than the nights at the club they had. She could trust him. He had never gone past any of her limits when playing, never pushed her beyond what she could take. He was very protective and supportive of her.

Dillon drove to Tracy's house, hoping maybe tonight would be the night. Maybe she would let him in. He didn't understand why she kept him at a distance. He could tell she enjoyed playing at the club with him, and she definitely was a submissive. The sex was great, but she never wanted anything more. This was one of the few times she had allowed him to pick her up. Usually, she met him wherever they were going, preferring to drive herself. Tonight he planned to hopefully change some of that.

The club had two suites for visitors, and he had gotten the okay to use one. Tonight there would be no sneaking off in the dark for Miss Tracy Smith. He was getting some answers, whatever it took.

He had done a little digging on Tracy, hoping to learn more about her, but couldn't find much. Her undocumented past bothered him. Everyone had a past, and with his computer skills, nothing was a secret. He was hitting a brick wall with Tracy. There was either nothing there or somebody had buried it very deep. With her job at the FBI, he should have been able to learn some piece of data, but every time he tried to go back further than five years, he found a blank. Nothing. No school history, no family, nothing. He asked Derek about it, and all Derek had told him was, "Talk to her," and he refused to tell him anything else. Derek wasn't like that. Miss Tracy was a mystery he was going to crack if it took the rest of his life.

When he pulled into her driveway, she was sitting on the steps waiting for him. She stood as she saw him pull in and was at the side of his truck before he got it stopped.

"I could have knocked. You shouldn't be out here," he admonished her. He knew she could protect herself, and the neighborhood looked safe enough, but the Dom in him needed to protect her. "You've earned a punishment for that."

"We're not even at the club yet. Knock it off." He could tell something was bothering her. Normally she was very respectful. Maybe she needed this s badly as he did.

"Don't push it, darling. I can play this game just as well as you can. You know what happens to brats in the club," he answered her, his eyes not leaving the road. She was being bratty just to get her way, a method of topping from the bottom and something he never tolerated.

Tracy was wearing a short dark-green skirt that matched her eyes, and an off-white tank top. Club wear, but something mild enough that she could also wear it outside to wait for him.

"Spread them. I want to make sure you followed my instructions." Dillon had sent her a text telling her how he wanted her prepared for their play tonight. If she had not complied, she was going to have a longer punishment session, and he really wanted to play, not punish, but she seemed to need a heavier hand tonight than normal.

Tracy slowly let her legs fall open, showing her shaved pussy and the fact she wasn't wearing underwear. She had followed his instructions to the letter. She knew better than to disobey.

"Come over here, darling, and I'll give you your reward and take the edge off for you," he crooned.

Tracy undid her belt and slid to the middle of the truck, using the belt there to restrain herself. She again let her legs fall open and closed her eyes in anticipation of what he would do.

Dillon took one finger and slowly traced the lips of her mouth with it. "Open and suck it." He pushed his finger into her mouth. She sucked it in and ran her tongue around it, mimicking what she wanted to do to his cock.

After swirling his finger around her mouth for a few minutes, he trailed it down to her cleavage. Briefly stopping there, he pinched each nipple through the fabric of her top. He continued his journey, slipping his fingers into the folds of her pussy, finding her wet and ready for him. Using her juices, he spread them to her clit. Then, still using just the one finger, he tapped her clit with just enough pressure to bring her to boiling.

He stopped just before she could come and heard her groan of frustration. "If you behave, when we get to the club, I'll give you what you need, but you have to be good until we get there."

Tracy wasn't in the mood for this bullshit and didn't hesitate to tell him exactly what she thought of his plan. "Look, Dillon, just because I agreed to play with you doesn't mean you get to be the big bad Dom all the time. Lay off."

Dillon chuckled and looked at her briefly. "Baby, you can bitch all you want, but it all boils down to 'obey or don't come.' I'll get what I need either way. You're only hurting yourself." She really was in a mood tonight. This was one of the few times she had allowed him to pick her up, and now he knew why. She obviously wanted some extra attention tonight.

Tracy sat pouting. She really, really liked Dillon. She could tell he wanted more and wished she could give it. Her heart knew that Dillon would never hurt her like *He* had. She couldn't convince her mind yet. Maybe tonight she would tell him about her past, the part of her no one but Derek and some of her supervisors knew.

Dillon was the perfect man in her opinion, tall at six feet two inches, with short black hair and the bluest eyes she had ever seen. He was also very strong. He had won the strength category in the FBI competitions several years running. The man could bench-press a Toyota.

Always the perfect Dom, he knew exactly what she needed when she needed it. He had never pushed her too far and always managed to stop at just the right time. Her orgasms were out of this world, and the sex was just what she needed. If she had only met him first, how different things might be.

Maybe she should trust him more. He had proved himself several times in the club, and there was no reason to fear him.

They arrived at the club, and Dillon helped her from the truck and escorted her in. Separating to use the locker rooms, they reunited at the bar. Link, Dillon's friend, coworker, and part owner of the club, was at the bar, and the men were talking when Tracy walked up. Tracy and Link were also friends and had worked on the same assignments several times. Tracy looked to Dillon for permission to talk. Once she saw his slight nod, she greeted Link and spoke with several people she knew sitting at the bar, before Dillon led her off.

"What are you in the mood for tonight?" he asked. He didn't always give her the option, and just because he asked didn't mean she would get her way, but he wanted some indication of how much she needed.

Taking a deep breath, she reminded herself that this was okay, that she could trust Dillon in private. She clutched his hand and answered, "Let's go to a private room. I want something a little more intense tonight."

Dillon squeezed her hand back and walked with her to the area for the private rooms. "Do you want a theme room?" he asked, still giving her the choice to back out if she needed to.

"You choose," was all she could manage to answer.

Dillon could feel her trepidation in the way her hand shook in his and by the look on her face and was impressed that she would give him as much control as she did. In the past, she had always kept control of the scene by deciding where and how they would play, and he had let her have that. Tonight she was giving him more of herself, and he planned to cherish everything she would let him have.

Dillon grabbed the key to one of the suites, glad he had reserved it earlier. The night was working out the way he wanted. He hadn't planned a scene and wasn't ready to take her to a theme room, but if she'd wanted that, he would have improvised something quickly. They would do that another night. Walking her to the room he had reserved, he could feel her relax when she saw where they were.

He led her into the room and locked the door. Tonight he wanted privacy. She didn't need to be on display.

"Strip," he commanded her as he set his toy bag down and grabbed some water from the small fridge. Sitting in the overstuffed chair, he watched her as she undressed. When she was finished, she stood before him, hands clasped behind her back, feet shoulder width apart, head down, waiting for his next instruction.

"Kneel," he said.

She did as he commanded, eyes still on the floor.

Spreading his legs wide, he indicated for her to move forward and kneel between them. When she was in the correct position, he lifted her chin with one finger to look into her eyes.

"You are so beautiful." He raised a bottle of water to her lips.

She drank gratefully. Her mouth had become very dry. Tracy was very nervous being in a private setting again, even though she had played with Dillon several times. The last time she was with a man in a private place, she'd almost been killed.

Dillon could see the anxiety in her eyes and had to learn what was bothering her. Pulling her up to sit in his lap, he started smoothing his hand up and down her naked back in a calming motion. "Tell me who hurt you, Tracy. Who made you like this?" he asked her quietly. He had tried to talk to her before, but she had always closed him off. He hoped this time would be different.

Dillon felt if he could get Tracy to talk, it would be a major step in their relationship. Keeping his hand moving over her silky skin in a soothing motion, he encouraged her to open up to him.

"It happened a long time ago." Tracy took a deep breath, steadying herself before she started. "I was young, just out of college, and thought I owned the world until I met *Him. He* was older than I was, by several years, and had been in the lifestyle for a long time. *He* had just released his last slave when I met him at a club. I hadn't been going there long and was just starting to explore BDSM. I wasn't sure it was what I wanted, you know?"

She looked deep into his eyes. Not wanting to interrupt her, he nodded, letting her continue her story.

"We were introduced by friends of mine, people I trusted. Things started slowly at first. *He* took the classes the club offered for new submissives with me and was the perfect gentleman. After several months, *He* asked me to move in with him, and we progressed into a twenty-four/seven total power exchange after we had been living together for about a year. At this point, we had been together for two years. I didn't breathe without his permission.

"At first, everything was good, and we were very happy. I went back to college and started pursuing a degree in criminal justice, and *He* supported us. I didn't have to work and could concentrate on my studies. My only responsibility was to him and my schoolwork. I did all the cooking, cleaning, and anything else he needed.

"After a couple more years, *He* started to get restless. Suddenly, nothing I did was good enough. The punishments were harsher, and *He* had to take me to the emergency room several times. I don't know what *He* told them, but *He* never got in any trouble, until the last time. I came very close to leaving him, but *He* always convinced me that he would change. This lasted almost a year. I had nowhere to go. I wasn't working and had nothing of my own. The house, the cars, the bank accounts were all in his name. I had nothing."

A tear slipped down her face at this point, and Dillon kissed it off, still staying quiet to encourage her to continue her story. Looking into his eyes and smiling, she took a deep calming breath and went on.

"Things continued to get worse between us, and *He* started leaving me alone more and more, which was fine. I had begun to dread the time *He* was home, and when *He* was gone, he wasn't hurting me. One night, *He* came home drunk and in a rage. We had been together almost five years at this point, and it was my twenty-seventh birthday. *He* beat me so bad I awoke in the hospital with severe lacerations and several broken bones. He broke my arm in two places, I had several broken and cracked ribs, my collarbone was broken, and he whipped me so bad that I had to have plastic surgery on my back to cover the scars." She was sobbing by this point and turned her face to bury it in Dillon's shoulder.

After crying for a few minutes, she calmed herself and pulled away from him. Dillon started to stop her, but she put a finger across his lips. "Let me finish. If I don't, I may not have to courage to start again," she said softly.

"I pressed charges, and *He* was put in jail. *He* made several threats against me, and the police finally decided I needed to be put in protective custody. I changed my name and moved here. The only other people who know my story are Derek and some of the supervisors. I know *He's* still in jail. I get regular updates from my lawyer, and if he is ever released, I will be notified. I've tried to put it behind me, but as you can see, I still have that fear. I know you are nothing like him, but *He* wasn't like that at first. That's my fear. That I will find someone nice and he will turn on me. I can't go through that again. No one knows where I am. I can't contact any of my old friends or family for fear he might find me." She was sobbing again, and Dillon held her tight and let her cry.

Tracy finally pulled herself together again and shifted away to look at him. "I know you aren't him and you would never hurt me as *He* did. I know you want different things, and I also know you want more. I think I do, too. It's hard for me to trust. It's hard to let go. The only time I feel safe is when I'm alone. I want to feel safe with you. How can I do that?"

Dillon didn't know how to answer her. He wanted her to feel safe with him too. He was glad to hear she wanted more but wasn't sure what to say or how to reassure her.

"Thank you for sharing that with me. You went through a horrible experience. I wish I had the words to assure you that I. Will. Never. Do. Anything. Like. That. What that man did was abuse your trust, and he wasn't a Dom."

"I realize that now, but I was young and had just begun exploring who I was. I learned many hard lessons." Tracy took another deep breath and slipped her arms around his neck. "Can we play now? I really want to," she said as she leaned up to kiss him. She could feel his erection beneath her and could tell he was ready also. She'd been sitting naked in his lap this entire time.

Dillon realized this was the change he had been waiting for. This was what they needed to move their relationship forward, and it meant a lot that she was ready.

"Okay, let's play. First, you get a punishment for being bratty in the truck," he told her as he lifted her off his lap and stood with her. "On the bed, on your back. Arms over your head and legs spread," he told her as he turned to get his toy bag. All the rooms had wardrobes with equipment in them, but he preferred to use his own. He had bought things, especially for Tracy.

Turning with the toys he'd selected in his hands, he laid them on the bed before removing his shirt, shoes, and socks. He left his black leather pants on but unfastened them, giving his cock a little relief. Crawling up onto the bed, he straddled her hips and leaned down, rubbing her nipples with his chest.

Taking her mouth in a bruising kiss, he then reached up and fastened her wrists to the headboard. Kissing and licking his way down her body, he shifted himself down so he could also restrain her legs by fastening her ankles to the footboard.

"Too tight?" he asked, running two fingers around each restraint and knowing they weren't.

"No, I'm green, Master," she answered with a heavy sigh. She really did need this.

They hadn't played in several weeks, and the energy and frustration levels had been building in her. It was affecting their work together. She had been bitchy and bratty with him for no reason, and recently they had messed up on an important case because she was arguing with him. She couldn't let that happen again. Maybe now that she had told him her story, things would be different. They had to be. She couldn't go on as she had been. She needed more out of life. It had been long enough, and it was time to go on. She wanted a family and a life. She was sure she could find that with Dillon, and she thought he wanted that too.

Chapter Two

Dillon knelt between Tracy's wide-splayed legs and looked at the feast spread before him. No matter how often he saw her like this, he responded every time. She was gorgeous. Her body was lush and full, not skinny like so many of the girls nowadays. She wasn't heavy but had curves in all the places he liked them. Her breasts were like ripe fruit, his for the picking, and fit his large hands as if made for him. Her body was not hard and angled, but curved and soft and fit with his. She was short enough when standing that her head rested on his shoulder as if they were two puzzle pieces made to fit together. He wanted her.

Reaching for the nipple clamps he had set on the bed with the other toys, he showed them to her. "Remember these?"

She licked her lips in anticipation. She really did need this, and the bite of pain from the clamps was ideal.

"What are your safe words, Tracy?" He knew she would never have to use them with him but wanted to remind her that she had them if needed.

"Purple to slow down and orange to stop, Master," she answered. Most people used the stoplight system of red, yellow, and green, but Tracy liked purple and orange.

"Very good." He leaned down and took one nipple into his mouth, licking and sucking until it was ready for the clamp. Once he had it the way he wanted it, he swiftly applied the clamp, twisting it until he saw her wince. Then he did the same with the second clamp.

Tonight he had a surprise for her. He had a butterfly clamp he was going to put on her clit. They hadn't used one before, and he wasn't sure how she would respond. Showing it, he watched her eyes widen.

"We haven't used this before. I got it special for tonight."

Backing down her body, he lifted her clit to his mouth and began licking and sucking. She was wet and ready, her little clit shiny and swollen, needy.

Her body undulated, unable to resist—asking for more. They had played often enough that he knew her body well and what it needed and responded to. He could tell tonight, she needed more. Tonight was going to be very intense for them. It marked a change in their relationship, and each knew it.

Applying the clamp, he started it vibrating at the lowest speed. Then he grabbed the lube and a large butt plug, bigger than anything he had used on her in the past.

"I went shopping today. Look what I got for you," he bragged, holding up the plug where she could see it. He had hoped for more tonight and had gone shopping because of it.

"Oh my God, that's huge." She wiggled in anticipation. It was larger than anything she had ever had inside her but still not as large as he was.

"I need to stretch you. I will take this ass tonight." He had used several toys with her but never had taken her anally. He was sure she was ready.

Applying the lube, he teased her for several long minutes before he began slowly pushing the huge plug home. Watching her face for any signs of pain, he applied steady pressure until it was fully inserted. When he had the plug seated in her ass, he moved up her body to kiss her mouth.

"Are you still doing good, baby?" he asked against her lips.

"Yes, Sir, everything is good," she answered breathily, arching her torso to rub her clamped nipples against the soft hair on his chest. She loved that Dillon wasn't ashamed of his body. He was firm and muscular, but not so tough that he didn't cuddle. Some nights the best part of the scene was the aftercare. He was thoughtful, kind, and considerate. He always made sure she got what she needed. Tracy wondered why she had taken so long to explore more with him. She had known she could trust him a long time and could tell he had wanted more for just as long. All that time wasted. A tear slipped down her cheek.

"What's the matter, baby? Does something hurt?" Dillon asked, concerned. He had never seen that look on her face, and Tracy never cried during a scene. She might cry from release at the end, but never during. He was glad she had decided to tell him her story tonight but wished she had told it to him before. It answered many of his questions and explained countless things. Had he known, he wouldn't have pushed her as he had sometimes and would have been more understanding of her needs. He thought about undoing the restraints and holding her but could tell she needed him to continue. He would have her in his arms soon enough, time to give his girl what she wanted.

Leaning down, he licked the tear, then placed his mouth over hers, slipping his tongue between her lips and exploring her sweet depths. Bracing himself on his forearms, he crouched over her and rubbed her slit with his firm, hard dick, bumping her clit and the clamp. He knew this still wasn't enough for her, so he lifted himself off her and went to get the first of two floggers he would use on her.

Walking back to her, twirling the flogger, he stopped by the side of the bed and let it drift over her clamped nipples, gradually increasing the speed and pressure until he was striking both breasts fairly fast and he could see her skin begin to redden. He saw her body give and the euphoria begin to flow over her. She was drifting off into subspace, where she needed to be.

Pausing long enough to straddle her again, he grabbed the second flogger; this would be much more intense. Tracy had beautiful breasts, and they were firm and full. Her nipples were very sensitive. She loved having them clamped and flogged. They had played with rope often, and she was very responsive when he wrapped her breasts. He hadn't planned that for tonight and hoped the floggers and the paddle would be enough. He also had a paddle he would use on her ass, thighs, and breasts.

Her breasts were beginning to turn red, and Dillon knew it was time to give them a rest. "Okay, baby, that's enough on your beautiful tits for now. Let's see what we can do on your little bottom. Time to flip you over."

This time Dillon arranged her so she was bent over the side of the bed with her bottom sticking up in the air. She would be lying on her breasts, which would intensify the experience for her. He fastened her hands straight out over her head and left her feet loose but widespread on the side of the bed. Making sure he hadn't stretched her too tight, he added a couple of pillows under her hips to raise her higher. Then he stepped back to make sure she was at the right height for what he had planned.

Warming her up with his hands, he first squeezed both globes of her ass firmly several times until they started to warm and redden slightly. He then stepped between her legs and rubbed himself in her slit several times, again bumping the vibrating clamp on her clit. He also twisted the plug and pumped it in and out a few times.

He stepped back again and grabbed his thick flogger with wide, firm straps. This would sting and redden her nicely for the paddle.

When she was moaning loudly with each impact, he stopped and grabbed the paddle. "Baby, I'm going to give you ten with a paddle for your brattiness in the truck. This will be your punishment."

The paddle could bruise if used incorrectly, but he was going to make sure it didn't happen. He wanted her to be uncomfortable for a day or two but have no lasting marks. He used a heavier hand with the paddle than he normally would, but it was a punishment, not play.

Tracy let out a little scream with the first stroke of the paddle. He normally didn't hit that hard. "Ohhh shit, that hurt," she said with a groan.

"It's a punishment, little one. It wasn't supposed to feel good," Dillon told her with a chuckle in his voice.

Tracy normally would have bristled at someone calling her "little one," but coming from Dillon tonight, it was more a term of affection than an insult. Tracy wasn't short for a woman, at five feet six inches, but all the men she worked with were taller than her, and she was constantly getting called "short stuff," "shrimp," "little one," and anything thing else they could come up with to symbolize her stature. She was only 130 pounds, and some of the men had even called her dainty. That was until they met her on the gym floor. She had a black belt in several martial arts, was an expert street fighter, and had taken boxing lessons as well. When she had left *Him*, she decided that she would never be in a position where she couldn't defend herself again. All the effort she had put in had served her well in her work for the FBI.

"Okay, Tracy, that was one. I need you to count these next ten and tell me why you need this." Dillon slapped his hand over the place the paddle had marked.

"Yes, Sir, I was bratty in the truck and didn't show the proper respect," she answered him.

"Very good, now we proceed with your ten." And he did. Alternating sides and varying the intensity, he continued until she was sobbing and just managed to get out the word "ten."

Grabbing the cream he always kept in his bag, he immediately started rubbing it into her flaming skin, knowing the sooner he treated her the faster she would heal and the less bruising she would have. Once he had sufficient cream rubbed into her skin, he leaned over her, rubbing his throbbing dick into the cleft of her buttocks.

"I'm going to take this ass now, baby. Relax and let me inside," he said, licking the shell of her ear before turning her head enough to take her lips.

Releasing the kiss left them breathless. He grabbed a condom and quickly put it on. He slowly removed the plug from her and added a large amount of lube to her gaping hole. Using three fingers, he spread the lube, then placed some on his condom-covered cock.

Slowly he started pushing himself into her tight warmth, using all the self-control he had to keep from ramming himself into her. Once he got his mushroom-shaped head past the ring of nerves there, he stopped and leaned over her, licking the shell of her ear.

"How are you doing, baby? Are you good?" he whispered, still holding himself in check.

Tracy couldn't believe how this was making her feel. The experience was primitive, more deep and dark than anything she had ever experienced. The connection she felt to Dillon was deeper than anything she had ever felt with anyone. When *He* had tried to take her ass, it hurt so bad, and there had been so much blood, that he had to take her to the emergency room. Tracy didn't know what kind of story he made up that time, but there were never any questions asked. This experience with Dillon was totally different.

She had known that Dillon wanted to try this with her for a long time, but always put him off. She had never told him the truth about why she was so worried about what he wanted to do. Now she was glad she had trusted him enough to allow him to use her body this way. Having him this way was the most extreme erotic connection she had ever felt with another person.

"Dillon, I'm good. This is...I don't have words to describe what you're doing to my body."

"Just relax, baby. I'm going to push in a little more now," Dillon told her as he leaned down and took the skin at the back of her neck between his teeth. Slipping one hand beneath her, he started flicking her clit back and forth by the clamp. He would have to remove the clamps soon; they had been on long enough.

Using one hand, he reached up and unfastened her arms, then grasped her around the waist and lifted her, not losing the connection between them. Still holding her, he sat on the side of the bed with her back to his front and began slowly lifting her hips up and down on him. When he could tell by the sounds she was making she was close, he reached around and removed one of the nipple clamps, and she came screaming his name. Before she had come all the way down from that orgasm, he removed the other nipple clamp, sending her right back up to the moon. Then, using both hands, he massaged both her nipples, helping bring the blood back to them.

Tracy leaned back against Dillon, tears running down her face. They weren't tears of pain or sadness, but the opposite. They were tears of release. The release of all the tension she had been holding all these years. Tears for the person she used to be, tears for the girl who had been abused. Tracy liked to think she had gotten over all that she had been through, but the truth was she hated the lie she had been living. It felt good being able to trust someone who cared for her again, and she could tell Dillon cared for her. She had missed so much not trusting anyone, but especially not trusting him. Time to make some changes in her life again. Time to let Dillon help her.

"You haven't," Tracy said to Dillon in a soft voice. She could sense that he hadn't found his release yet and wanted him to be as happy as she was.

"I will, baby. I want to be in that tight pussy of yours when I come. Just enjoy." Dillon moved her long dark-auburn hair over one shoulder. Her hair was so long that she could sit on it. Normally she kept it braided for work, but when they were playing, she left it long for him. He scraped his teeth along the spot where her neck met her shoulder, knowing this was a very sensitive spot for her.

Tracy shuddered and felt his cock jump in her ass. That and what he was doing to her neck was enough for her to start the climb again. Was this three or four? She had lost count of the number of orgasms he'd given her.

"Okay, baby, time to switch," Dillon told her as he once again flipped them so she was now lying on her back. He quickly removed the condom he had on and handed a fresh one to Tracy to put on for him.

Looking into his eyes for permission, Tracy took the condom and put it in her mouth. One of her girlfriends had taught her this trick years ago, to put a condom on a man with her mouth, and Dillon loved it.

Pushing him over onto his back, she crawled down his body until she was in position. Taking his throbbing erection into her mouth, she used her tongue to put the condom on him, allowing him deep down her throat in the process. She smiled around him when she heard his groan. He loved it when she took him that far back. Lifting up, she kissed, licked, and nibbled her way up his body until she was lying across him.

Dillon put his hands on her shoulders and flipped her onto her back, widening her legs with his to make a place for himself. Turning up the speed on the butterfly one last time, he slowly pushed his cock into her tight pussy. "Next time, I'll take you with the plug in your ass." He wanted to do it this time but was afraid she would be too sore. After they had rested, he was going to take her to soak in the tub and rub more cream onto her ass. He didn't want her to hurt too bad the next day. He wanted her to enjoy the experience and want to do it again and again.

Slowly pushing until he was all the way in, he reached down and pulled the clamp off her clit, causing her to come with a scream. He set a fast pace and thrust himself rapidly in and out until he came, groaning her name, and collapsed on her for a few brief moments.

Rolling to the side and pulling her with him, he pulled a blanket over them. "Rest for a while, baby. Then we'll take a hot bath before I take you home." He hoped she would let him stay with her. They had never spent more than a few hours together, and he wanted to awaken with her in his arms.

Chapter Three

Tracy woke with Dillon carrying her to the already steaming tub. He must have filled it while she was still sleeping.

Noticing her stirring in his arms, he brushed a kiss across her forehead and said, "We're going to soak for a while. Then I'll take you home. How's that sound?"

Nestling closer to him and settling her head on his shoulder, she smiled and answered, "That sounds wonderful," turning her head to place little kisses across his shoulder and neck.

Dillon settled them in the bath, and they soaked for a while. He took her out of the tub and wrapped them each in large warm towels before carrying her back to the bedroom. He carefully applied cream to all the areas he thought might bother her before helping her dress for the ride home.

Slipping one arm around her, he walked her to his truck. "Do you want to stop for something to eat before we go home?" he asked her, trying to decide how to ask to stay the night.

"No, I'll get something when I get home. Are you hungry? I could fix something for us." She wanted to ask him to stay but wasn't sure she was ready for that.

"Sure, I'll help, and we'll do it together," he told her with a smile.

They were quiet for the rest of the ride, lost in their thoughts. Once at her house, they worked together to fix a light meal. It was late, and they were tired. It had been an intense evening for them.

Dillon had been to Tracy's house a few times, but never for long. Usually, she met him at the door, and off they went. He liked it. Her house reflected her personality. She had a great deal of Southwest influences, without them being overstated. When he complimented her on it, she explained that her grandfather on her father's side was part Cherokee Indian, and it had influenced her tastes.

Dillon smiled. That also explained her darker coloring. They enjoyed the meal together, and then Tracy led him to the living room. Sitting on the couch, Tracy curled up next to him and pulled a light throw over her legs.

"This is nice. Why haven't we done this before?" she asked, snuggling closer to him.

"I don't know. I could get used to this." He pulled her even closer.

They sat for a while and listened to the music Tracy had started when they walked into the room. Dillon noticed she was dozing off and pulled her into his arms. "Come on, let's get you to bed. It's late, and you've had a hard night," he said, standing with her in his arms and heading to where he hoped the bedrooms were.

Tracy roused enough to direct him to her bedroom and wrapped her arms around his neck as he laid her in the bed. "Stay," she whispered sleepily. "I want you to stay."

"Are you sure you won't regret this in the morning?" he asked, afraid to hope she really did want him to stay.

"Yes, I don't want to be alone tonight," she answered him, pulling him closer.

"Okay, let me go make sure the house is locked up, and I'll be right back." There was no way he was going to pass up this opportunity. He quickly ran out to his truck and grabbed his gun, not that he would need it, but he never slept without one close. You never knew. Then running back into the house, he made sure everything was locked before going back to Tracy.

Stripping everything off, he crawled naked into the bed with her and proceeded to undress her. When she was naked, he pulled her to spoon with him and covered them both.

Tracy woke the next morning after the best sleep she had ever had. Ever since she had left *Him*, she hadn't felt safe. Sleeping in Dillon's arms had changed that. Looking around, she didn't see Dillon, but his side of the bed was still warm, so he hadn't been gone long. She got out of bed and, after a quick detour to take care of some necessities, grabbed a robe and headed to the kitchen, where something smelled wonderful.

Standing in her kitchen, barefoot and shirtless, was one gorgeous hunk of man. The fact he was wielding a spatula and dancing around to some song in his head made the sight all the better. Tracy stood silently for a few minutes watching him. He was apparently unaware she was there.

Dillon heard noises from Tracy's bedroom and knew she was awake. He was so happy he didn't care how he looked as he danced to some song playing in his head. He hoped she didn't mind, but he had found everything for omelets and made some coffee for himself and tea for her. He knew she didn't drink coffee. He had planned to bring her breakfast in bed, then play a little, but he could make this work too. He was a fast thinker and faster on his feet.

Spinning around, he danced over and grabbed her around the waist, lifting her off her feet and twirling her around. "Good morning, sunshine. Sleep well?" he asked and took her mouth in a passionate kiss that left her breathless.

Before she could answer, he set her on a barstool at the island in her kitchen and went back to whatever he had on the stove. "That smells delicious. What is it?" she asked, practically drooling over the aroma of what he was cooking.

"My secret omelet recipe, very few people are privileged enough to try one. Consider yourself special." He smiled and flipped the egg concoction expertly onto a plate. Adding hash browns and toast, he carried a plate to her with a cup of tea already prepared the way she liked it, three sugars and cream.

Tracy took a sip of the tea and pronounced it "perfect" before taking a forkful of the eggs. "There is no way I had all this in my kitchen." She was amazed at what he had done.

"I had to scrounge, but you did have what I needed. I need to take you to the store, though. I used most of what was in your fridge making this," he told her and leaned down to nibble her neck. He couldn't believe how little food she had in her house. What did the woman eat? They would talk about this later.

Tracy sat back on the stool and sipped her tea again. A girl could get used to something like this. She couldn't remember ever seeing Dillon in a mood like this, and she was happier than she had been in a long time.

They finished breakfast, and Dillon led her to the shower. Dillon started the water to warm, then turned and took Tracy in his arms. Using one hand to hold the back of her head, he gently parted her lips with his before moving his hand down to slip the robe off her shoulders. He turned stepped away and pushed his jeans down. Tuning back to Tracy, he lifted her and stood her in the shower before joining her.

Lifting the shower wand, he rinsed both of them before grabbing the body wash and squirting a small amount in his hands. Turning her back to him, he rubbed his hands together and starting with her shoulders began to was and massage her back, letting his hand slide down to cup each buttock. Then he slid his hands down her legs, picking each foot up and washing each toe.

Turning her, he again applied soap to his hands, soothing them down her chest to her breasts. Taking each breast in one hand, he swirled the soap round and round before pinching each nipple. Adding more soap, his hands drifted down to her pussy, parting her folds and running his fingers up and down her slit, before stopping to pinch and pull her clit. He stopped just before she could come.

"My turn," he told her, handing her the body wash and leaning against the shower wall. Tracy washed him as thoroughly as he did her. When she finished, he turned her and bent her over, hands resting on the seat in the shower before he took her from behind. Before then, showering had been purely functional for Tracy. Dillon made it an erotic experience. She would never see her shower the same way again.

After their long, leisurely shower, Dillon picked out the clothes she was to wear for the day, and then they headed for his condo. Tracy had never seen his place, and Dillon wanted to show it to her. He was more comfortable there and had more provisions than she did. He talked her into packing a bag to stay the night. They didn't have to be at work until Monday, and he wanted to spend the weekend with her. He was afraid to let her be alone—afraid she would change her mind about them. He didn't want to lose what ground they had made.

Tracy was still nervous but felt more relaxed than she had in a long time. This was the right thing to do. She could trust Dillon.

When they arrived at his house, he showed her around and helped her get settled before asking, "What do you want to do today, beautiful?"

Tracy didn't have to think long before answering him. "How about we just relax and watch movies or something like that? I'd really like to spend time getting to know you and telling you more about my past."

They spent the day talking, laughing, and enjoying each other's company. Finally, it started getting late, and Tracy was tired. She had been curled up in Dillon's lap on the sofa, watching an old movie with him, but could barely keep her eyes open anymore. Sitting up and grabbing his hand, she pulled him up behind her.

"Let's go to bed. I'm wiped."

Dillon understood—it had been an emotional couple of days for her—and followed her to the bedroom. They got ready for bed and undressed, crawling in together.

Tracy turned onto her side facing Dillon and kissed him gently. "Do you want to?" she asked him, scooting closer so their bodies were touching. She could tell he was aroused, but other than some passionate kisses and gentle petting, he had done nothing sexual all day.

"Not if you're too tired. This isn't about sex. I want us to have a real relationship, and I want to meet all of your needs, not just the sexual ones." He wrapped her in his arms and pulled her closer as he rolled to his back, pulling her to lie over him. "Let's just sleep for now; I may wake you later with a surprise." He settled her where he wanted, and she wiggled to get comfortable. Then he pulled a blanket over them and lay there content, holding her.

Tracy woke in the dark to find Dillon fulfilling his promise. She was flat on her back with him caged over her, slowly thrusting inside her. "Oh, that's so good," she moaned, closing her eyes again and just drifting in the sensations. She could definitely get used to this and to Dillon.

Dillon leaned down and took one of her nipples into his mouth as he sped up his thrusting, bringing each the release they needed. Lying back on his side, he pulled Tracy to him, fitting her body to his.

"Go back to sleep now, baby. It's the middle of the night, but I couldn't resist you any longer." He nuzzled her neck and held her closer.

Tracy felt her body relax and let go, wondering if it were all a dream. It seemed too good to be true.

Tracy woke again in the daylight to the most wonderful smells drifting into the room. Getting up, she grabbed one of Dillon's shirts and went to investigate. Finding her way to the kitchen, she walked into the room and asked, "What is that? It smells wonderful," when Dillon turned around.

"It's a casserole my mother makes for us when the family gets together. It has a little of everything in it. Ham, bacon, sausage, eggs, hash browns, peppers, and onions. It's about done. Have a seat; I have your tea ready." Dillon wasn't a tea drinker himself but kept some in the house for visitors, secretly hoping he could serve it to Tracy sometime. Today he was glad he did.

Tracy sat, giving a little screech when the cold wood touched her bare bottom. She had just grabbed the shirt and nothing else, and even though it was long on her, it pulled up when she sat, baring her bottom.

Dillon gave a little chuckle when he set the plate in front of her. "Cold, baby?" he asked with a big grin on his face.

Tracy looked for something to throw but, finding nothing, settled for punching him instead. "Be nice," she told him.

"Oh, baby, that was nice. There are so many other things I could have and will do," he told her. The grin on his face now looked evil.

Tracy shuddered and took a quick sip of her tea, looking down at her plate. This was going to be more fun than she had ever imagined. Dillon was nothing at all like *Him*.

They made quick work of breakfast, and since Dillon had done the cooking, Tracy volunteered to clean up. Once everything was done and put back in its place, Dillon asked what she wanted to do for the day.

"How do you feel about the flea market? I love going there, and it's fun to bum around," she asked him.

"Sounds good. Let's get dressed and head out there. It's supposed to be nice today. It will probably be crowded." Dillon grabbed her by the hand and led her to the bedroom, where they could get dressed.

Tracy dressed casually in shorts, tank top, and tennis shoes, wanting to be comfortable for the day and a little sexy for Dillon.

When she walked out to the living room, Dillon's jaw dropped. Twirling around, she giggled and asked, "Too much?"

"No, perfect. So perfect, how would you like to stay home and play?" he asked, wiggling his eyebrows.

Throwing her arms around his neck, she gently brushed his lips with hers and didn't resist when he took over. She melted into his embrace and let him take control.

Dillon cupped both ass cheeks with his hands and lifted until Tracy wrapped her legs around him. Moving slowly, he walked until he had her braced against the nearest wall, still exploring her mouth with his. Holding her tighter, he slipped one hand under the back of her tank top, running his hand up her bare back. Pulling away from her, he mouthed, "No bra?" giving her a minute to answer before taking her mouth again.

Tracy just smiled and nodded in answer to his question, threading her fingers through his hair to pull him closer. "I don't need one with this top," she whispered before he took her mouth again.

Dillon moved his hand around her until he was rubbing her nipple back forth with his thumb and adjusted her so he was rubbing his cock against her crotch, mimicking what he wanted to do without the clothes.

When he finally broke the kiss, they were each panting with need. "Are you sure you want to go out?" he asked.

Tracy thought for a minute before answering him. "As much fun as this is, how about I make it up to you when we get home?" She moved her legs down until she was standing on her own feet.

"I'll hold you to that," Dillon answered her as he took her mouth again.

Tracy relaxed into the kiss for a minute before she pushed him back and ducked under his arm to grab her bag. If they didn't leave soon, she would never get him from the house.

She was happier than she had been in a long time. She realized this was what she had been missing. Someone she cared about that cared for her. Someone to have fun with and who didn't care what they did when. When she had been with *him*, he had controlled everything, and that had been what she thought she wanted. Now she realized a 24/7 relationship would never work for her. She was too independent for that. She loved submitting in the bedroom and in play but needed to be her own person the other times.

It had been five years since she left *him*, and it was time to love and trust again.

She grabbed Dillon's hand and pulled him out the door. They were going to have fun.

Dillon drove them to the flea market. They spent most of their time walking around and looking at the various exhibits. Tracy found a few things, and they had some bags to carry by the time they made it to the concession stands. Dropping her bags and flopping down at an empty table, she pulled Dillon down beside her.

"Aren't you tired yet?" she asked breathlessly. It was hot, and she was wearing down.

"Oh no you don't, you promised me you would make it up to me when we got home. You are not tired," Dillon teased Tracy, grabbing her and pulling her in for a kiss.

"If you want me to keep that promise, I need food and drink before I fade away," she giggled back.

"Turkey legs and lemonade?" he asked.

"Perfect," she answered, fanning herself with a napkin.

Tracy kicked her legs out in front of her and leaned back, closing her eyes a minute while waiting for Dillon. Even though she was dressed for it, it was still a hot and muggy day. She must have drifted off for a minute, because next thing, she felt a hand on her shoulder.

"Miss, are you all right?" a strange voice asked.

She jumped and straightened up, looking around for the source of the voice. Just a kind-looking stranger. "I'm waiting for my friend; he went to get drinks and food. It's warm today," she answered, pulling herself together.

"Yes, it is." The stranger smiled and walked away.

Tracy looked for Dillon and saw he was still in the line, several people back. It was going to be a few more minutes. She waved and smiled at him but stayed where she was. The seating area was crowded, and tables were hard to find. People had already taken all except the chair she was sitting in and one other at the table. She put her bags in the lone chair, not wanting it to be taken too.

She grabbed her phone and checked messages, nothing new, then checked her e-mail. There was one from her attorney, reminding her that *he* was up for parole again and asking if she wanted to go to the hearing. Tracy hadn't gone to one of his hearings yet and had no intention of going now, but out of courtesy, her attorney kept her informed and always gave her the option. She wasn't really worried and had been assured he would never get out on parole, or if he did, he would never be able to find her.

Dillon appeared with the food and drinks, and they enjoyed it while relaxing for a few more minutes. "Do you know that man over there?" Dillon asked her quietly.

Tracy turned to look but didn't see anyone she knew, so she answered, "No, why?"

"He keeps watching you. Come on, let's go." Dillon started gathering their things.

"Okay, I'm sure it's nothing." Tracy tried to laugh it off. She was sure Dillon was overreacting but was ready to leave anyway, so she didn't argue.

They stopped at a few more shops on the way out until Dillon finally pulled her to one side. "You stay here. I'm going to see if I can learn why this asshat is following us." He started to walk off determinedly.

Tracy grabbed his arm to stop him and looked into his eyes. "Just leave it; it's probably nothing. Please, let's just go home. I still have a promise to make up to you." She smiled and ran one fingertip across his cheek until it rested on his lips.

He took the finger in his mouth and bit gently. "Fine, but if I see this jackass again, I'm finding out what is going on."

Tracy didn't respond as she grabbed his hand and pulled him toward the truck. It was definitely time to go home.

When they got home, Tracy pulled Dillon into a cool shower and gave him what she had promised and more. Falling into the bed giggling like kids, they wrapped themselves in each other and closed their eyes to nap for a few before getting up for dinner.

"We have to work tomorrow. Do you need anything from your house?" Dillon asked her while they were cleaning up the dinner dishes.

"Yeah, I thought I'd spend the night there," Tracy answered with a sigh.

"Okay, let me grab what I'll need, and I'll come with you," Dillon said.

"Oh, okay," Tracy said. She hadn't really thought about him coming with her but didn't mind it. Their relationship had changed, and it appeared Dillon wasn't playing anymore. *Well,* she thought, *I guess this is good. It's what I wanted.*

Tracy was quiet, thoughtful, on the way back to her place. Something didn't feel right, but she couldn't tell what it was. It wasn't Dillon. There was something else.

"What's the matter, baby?" Dillon asked, sensing her distress.

"I don't know. I'm just tired. You wore me out this weekend. I need to go back to work to rest." She smiled at him, running her hand up his leg to his crotch and cupping him.

"Yeah, and if you don't stop that, I'll wear you out more." He grinned evilly.

Tracy smiled back at him, then sighed. She wished she could tell what was wrong. Something was just off.

When they arrived at her house, her porch light was on. That was odd. She didn't remember turning it on and didn't have it on a timer, even though she should. She didn't say anything to Dillon about it. Her door was still locked, and everything else appeared normal in the house. She was sure she was just tired, but everything felt off. Little things, like her knickknacks she kept on a table beside the door, looked like they had been moved, but she couldn't tell.

She went to her bedroom, Dillon trailing behind. When she came to the door, she stopped. One of her dresser drawers was open. She never left them open. It was one of her pet peeves.

"Were you in here before we left?" she asked, thinking maybe Dillon had left it open.

"No, why?" He stood straighter. Something was going on.

"I never leave my drawers open," she answered, leaning back into him, a shiver suddenly running up her back. Had someone been in her house? Were they still there?

"Do you have a gun?" Dillon asked quietly.

Tracy nodded. She always kept one loaded in her bedside drawer. She never knew what could happen in her line of work.

"Where?" Dillon mouthed.

Tracy pointed and let him move her around behind him, and they walked stealthily to the bed. She reached around and showed him how to trigger the mechanism that would open the spring lock door only she (and now Dillon) knew about. The drawer opened with a click, and Tracy jumped, clinging to Dillon.

"Relax. If anyone was here, the person is probably long gone," he whispered.

"Then why are we being so quiet?" she asked in the same tone.

"Just in case." He grinned. Holding the gun with one hand and her with the other, he pulled her toward the bathroom, where he pushed the door open with his foot, checking the room to make sure it was empty. "Clear."

He checked the closet and under the bed, making sure no one was in the room. He led her through the house, thoroughly checking each room. When he was sure they were the only ones in the house, he pulled her to the living room and sat, pulling her into his lap.

"Did you see anything else out of place?" Dillon asked, holding her close.

"I didn't really look. Come on," she said, standing up and grabbing his hand.

Dillon thought of telling her it could wait, but he knew it couldn't, and neither would be happy until she checked everything again.

Dillon followed Tracy from room to room, watching as she looked carefully in each room, sometimes shaking her head and other times just looking confused. "Well?" he finally asked.

"Yes and no," she answered.

"What do you mean by that?" He was getting tired too.

"It looks like everything is here, but nothing seems like it is in the right place," she answered, plopping down on her bed. They had turned off lights and worked their way back to her bedroom.

Dillon sat and held her. They should have probably called the cops and had everything dusted for fingerprints, but it was too late now. Tracy had touched or moved everything. He knew better but let her anyway.

"Do you want to go back to my place? Would you feel safer there?" he asked, not sure what else he could do tonight.

"No, I'm afraid if I leave again, whomever it was might come back. I need a security system. I wonder if Tyler and the boys would come do one for me tomorrow?"

Tyler Thomas was a friend of theirs who also worked for the Secret Service and was a part owner of the Mix, the club they played at. He had recently retired and gotten married, but still did security work on the side for something to get him out of the house, as his wife Tammy was fond of saying.

"I'll call him now. It's still early. Let's see what he says." Dillon made the call quickly, and Tyler promised to be there early in the morning. Tracy and Dillon made quick calls to their bosses to let them know what was going on and to take a few days off. Neither was on assignment, so it was easy to get the time off.

Tracy relaxed somewhat knowing she would have the security installed as soon as possible and that Dillon would stay with her until they had finished.

They spent the evening talking about what Tracy wanted and needed to secure the house and whether she should just move in with Dillon, at least for now, which he was pushing for.

"I don't know," Tracy answered when he asked why she wouldn't move in with him for the fourth time. Part of her said it would probably be best, and part of her didn't want to give up her independence. He was slowly wearing her down, and she was close to giving in.

Dillon could tell he was pushing Tracy to the breaking point, but damn it, he wanted her in his bed and safe in his arms. He had waited so long to get her to this point that he couldn't stand the thought of losing her now. He could tell she was on the verge of giving in just to shut him up but feared to push too much harder. Maybe he needed to use a different form of persuasion.

Without saying a word, he grabbed her hand and pulled her up from the couch where she was sitting. Tracy let him pull her back to the bedroom; maybe if they were playing, he would stop bugging her about moving in with him.

When they got to the bedroom, he said the one word that got her body humming every time. "Strip."

While Tracy was quickly removing her clothes, Dillon got the bed ready. He removed the quilt and blankets. Then he added a scarf to each bedpost, checking to make sure they were secure. Without saying a word, he looked at her and nodded toward the bed.

Tracy quickly scrambled onto the bed and lay facedown. Dillon tapped one foot to get her attention and shook his head no. He wanted her lying on her back. Eyes wide, Tracy quickly scrambled onto her back wondering if he was going to talk at all.

Still not saying a word, Dillon pulled each of her arms over her head and wrapped the scarves from the bedposts around each of them, fastening them to the bed. Then he did the same thing with her ankles, which left her lying spread-eagle in the bed.

Moving off the bed, he walked the short distance to the dresser where he had placed his toy bag and took out his soft leather flogger.

Twirling the flogger as he walked up to Tracy, he looked at her. "The only words I want to hear from you are your safe words or the words 'Yes, Master Dillon, I think it's a good idea to stay with you.' No begging to come, and nothing else. Do you understand?"

Tracy nodded realizing now what was going to happen. He was going to tease her until she gave in. He wasn't going to let her come until he got his way.

Dillon wasn't sadistic, and Tracy knew he wouldn't hurt her. She was going to have as much fun as he was, but he was going to push her limits.

When Tracy nodded, Dillon stepped up to the side of the bed and started twirling the flogger over her breasts, barely brushing them at first, just enough to raise the sensitivity of the skin. After flogging her breasts for several minutes, he set the flogger aside and went back to his toy bag, his eyes never leaving her. Reaching into the bag, he brought out several clamps, a couple wide leather straps, and a riding crop. The crop looked somewhat like a flyswatter, but the end was smaller, only about an inch and a half wide and about two inches long.

Tracy knew exactly what it was for. He was going to use it on her breasts, her pussy, and, if she were lucky, her clit. Her temp rose about five degrees, and sweat beaded on her upper lip. This was going to be intense.

Standing by the side of the bed again, he placed the items he had taken from the bag on the bed next to her. "Remember, Tracy, you haven't been given permission to come, and you are to be silent. Understood?"

"Yes, Sir," she answered, eyes wide.

Dillon sat on the side of the bed and wrapped the wide leather straps around her upper thighs. Then he took one side of her labia and started applying the clamps to it. He placed three clamps evenly spaced on each of her labial lips, then threaded the small string from the straps through the clamps. Reattaching the string to the straps, he left her spread open and at his mercy. He leaned down and gently licked her clit, then blew a puff of his warm breath on it.

Tracy was sweating more now. If she came without his permission, she would be in trouble but could feel her body gearing up for its big moment.

Leaning over her, Dillon took one then the other nipple into his mouth and teased the peaks into hardness. Quickly he applied a clamp to each one, making sure they weren't too tight.

Then he took the crop and struck each nipple five times. He leaned over her and took her mouth in a scorching kiss, reaching down to barely brush her clit with his fingertips.

Pulling back from her, he looked into her eyes and asked, "Anything you want to say?"

Tracy shook her head no, thinking it would just be smarter to give in to him and agree, but now that she had put up a stand, she didn't want to give in easily.

"No?" Dillon asked, shaking his head. He straddled her so his pelvis was over her knees, took the crop, then started gently slapping the inside of her thighs with it, just hard enough to sting. After several slaps on her thighs, he started tapping her clit with the soft leather of the crop. He knew this wouldn't hurt but would increase the sensations she was feeling.

"Oh my God, Dillon, I can't take much more. Please?" Tracy couldn't help it. She was going to come, permission or not.

"No talking and no coming, girl. Understand?" Dillon said, tapping her clit harder with the crop. He could tell she was close, so close he didn't know how she was holding it back. *Time to intensify things a little,* he thought.

Reaching behind him, he grabbed the butt plug he had laid out and the lube. The plug was larger than any he had used before but still not as large as he was.

Holding the plug where she could see it, he slowly applied the lube to it. Lifting her up by the thighs, he propped a pillow under her, putting her little ass right where he wanted it.

Setting the plug on the towel he had laid out earlier, he picked up the crop again. "Do you know what I'm going to do now, baby?" He grinned evilly at her.

"Oh God, I can't take it." Tracy shuddered. Why didn't she just give in, her brain wondered, but her body was saying, *Go for it.*

Spreading her cheeks, Dillon took one finger and rimmed her little hole. "How do you think this is going to feel when the crop hits it? The burn, the heat, and then I'll put the plug in. After you've been properly prepared, I'm going to take you, Tracy. Are you ready for that?"

He leaned over her and, with his mouth hovering an inch over hers, said, "Say you'll come stay with me, baby, and I'll give you an orgasm like you've never had before." He was going to anyway, but she didn't need to know that now.

He leaned back and spread the cheeks of her ass with one hand while taking the crop with the other. Then he smacked her little brown hole, lightly, several times. This wasn't a punishment session. He just wanted his way.

When she felt the first strike, Tracy thought she was going to come. Biting her lip, she managed to pull herself back from the edge but didn't know how long she would be able to keep it up. Dillon struck her a few more times, then took his fingers and lubed her asshole, pushing them in and out, fucking her with his fingers. The more he did it, the more she moaned.

"Anything you want to tell me, darling, before I put the plug in and send you to the stars?" he asked while adding more lube to the plug.

Tracy bit her lip. She was stupid for not giving in, but this was fun in some ways, and she wanted to see what else he had up his sleeve.

"No?" he asked again, shaking his head. When she still didn't answer him, he slowly started pushing the plug into her ass.

Tracy noticed the burn and stretch more than she had before. Between the larger size of the plug and his smacking her with the crop, it had intensified her sensations back there.

"Oh God, Dillon. I...I...can't. I'm going to come," she screamed at him as she toppled over the edge to orgasm. Yelling his name, her body throbbed, and she tossed her head, overcome with the intensity of feelings.

Dillon took the crop and tapped her clit a few times, extending her orgasm on and on, until she was a breathless, sweaty mess.

"Oh God, I can't take anymore," Tracy panted as Dillon tapped her clit with the crop, her body arching, and thrashing. She screamed and cried, unable to control herself.

Finally, Dillon took pity on her and stopped everything, letting her body come down. He took a damp cloth and wiped her face and upper chest. Then he released her arms and sat her up, holding a bottle of water to her lips. Letting her drink her fill, he supported her until she relaxed.

"Okay, let me get all this off of you," he said as he laid her back down and started removing the clips from her pussy and the straps from her legs. Dillon gave her gentle kisses and pats as he unfastened her.

Tracy was so exhausted, she couldn't move. She lay there and let Dillon have his way.

When he had her free of all the straps and clamps, he raised her bottom and slowly worked the plug from her. He had planned on taking her anally again, but she was too wiped out for any more tonight. He had pushed her hard, and now she needed to rest.

Covering her with a light blanket, he kissed her forehead and went to run a bath for her. She needed a warm soak and to rest.

As he was carrying her to the bath, Tracy smiled up at him and said, "I give. I'll stay with you until we figure all this out."

Chapter Four

"Why, why, why did I ever give in to him?" Tracy asked herself for the fourth time as she carried another box into Dillon's house. She was moving a lot of stuff for something that was supposed to be temporary.

"Bring anything valuable," Dillon had said as she was packing. Even though they couldn't prove someone had been in her house, she agreed and packed all her mementos and valuables in boxes. Just the things she didn't want to be broken or stolen, she told herself. She hadn't realized she had accumulated this much stuff.

When she left *him*, she left so many things behind, things her parents had given her. The memories were still there, but knowing he had some of those things bothered her sometimes. When she told the counselors about those feelings, they answered, "Tracy, you don't know that he kept those things. You just need to go on." Nevertheless, it still bothered her sometimes.

What if she had to leave suddenly, and all of her things were at Dillon's house? She mentally shook herself. She couldn't think that way.

Dillon walked up and took the box from her hands to carry it to the room he had set up for storage. "Is this the last of it?" he asked.

"Yes, just my clothes are left," she replied.

He led her over to his brown leather couch. "Sit and rest. I'll get them." He could see the strain on her face and knew she really didn't want to stay there, but it made the most sense. His place was bigger, closer to their jobs, and unless someone was following her, no one would look for her here.

"Why don't you call Tyler and see how they are doing? Don't forget to have him route the camera feeds here." Dillon walked out the door.

Tracy did as he asked and was relieved to learn the security was almost done. She didn't like the idea of people being in her house when she wasn't home, and it didn't matter if it was people she knew. Dillon and Tyler had each insisted the job would get done faster if she was away, and Tyler even threatened to sic his very pregnant and cranky wife, Tammy, on her if she wouldn't leave.

She had been so busy planning with Dillon and trying to remember all she needed to pack, she hadn't taken the time to sit and think about whom could have broken into her house. She checked her e-mail to see if there was anything more from her attorney. It couldn't be *Him*. She knew he was still in jail. If he had been released, she would have been notified. She sent an e-mail to her attorney's office to notify them of the trouble she was having and to see if they had any information they hadn't passed along to her.

She was being silly and letting Dillon get to her. The fact someone had followed her around the flea market and that her house was broken into the same day were just coincidental. Feeling a shiver run over her, she jumped up to see whether she could help Dillon, needing the company of another person.

They worked together and got her things moved in. Dillon cleaned out a spare closet for her to store everything in. He wanted her in his bed but offered one of the spare rooms. He didn't want her to feel as if he was rushing her.

Tracy was grateful for the offer of her own room but wondered if he didn't want her for some reason. When bedtime came, she got her answer. Dillon took her hand and led her to the bedroom he had shown her earlier, stopping at the door; he took her in his arms and kissed her, showing her how much he wanted her.

"You can sleep in here, or you can come with me," he told her, not letting her go.

Tracy looked deep into his eyes and smiled. Nodding her head, she let him lead her to his room.

"Tonight we sleep, but it won't be that way every night, and I may wake you in the middle of the night," he said as they got ready for bed.

Tracy slipped to the bathroom to do what she needed and came out in one of her nightgowns, not sure how to dress for bed. She soon got her answer. Dillon was sitting on the side of the bed, naked, waiting for her.

"For as long as you sleep in my bed, it will be naked," he said to her, using his Dom voice.

Tracy walked over to him and allowed him to remove her gown, pulling it over her head. They were each so tired from moving and lying awake most of the night before that they were asleep almost as soon as their eyes closed.

Waking the next morning in Dillon's arms was nicer than Tracy expected it to be. When she was with *Him*, he expected her to be up before he was and to have breakfast ready and waiting. When she didn't, she paid for it. Dillon was nothing like him.

The next few days settled into a pattern, and Tracy told Dillon more about her life before, when she was Carrie. She told him about her family and people she missed since she had been unable to tell anyone what was happening or her new name. She really missed her mother and dad, but couldn't contact them when there was a chance he might learn where she was.

One night, at two in the morning, the alert tone on Dillon's phone sounded. Someone was in Tracy's house. The alarm automatically notified the police, but Dillon knew Tracy would want to be there too. Waking her, they dressed and quickly drove the short distance to her home. When they arrived the police were already there, but whomever it was had already left.

Tracy had been watching her e-mail daily for something from her attorney but had not received a reply. She told herself they were probably just busy, but something felt out of place. After a few more days, she decided to call them. She paid a large amount of money to keep them on retainer, and she was not going to be ignored.

Dillon was with her when she made the call. "Oh, Ms. Smith, Mr. Hall has been trying to reach you. I'll put you right through," the receptionist said when she answered.

"Tracy, Scott Hall here, thank God you called in. Your e-mail and phone have been hacked into. Are you safe?" he asked hurriedly.

"Yes, I'm safe. What's going on, Scott?" she asked with a sigh. She had been afraid something was going to happen. Things had been too quiet and were getting too comfortable. She walked with the phone to where Dillon was sitting and sat in his lap, needing to feel his protection. Slipping the phone into speaker mode, she nodded at Dillon to listen.

"Tracy, I've been trying to reach you to let you know *He* was granted parole," Scott said quietly into the phone. "The police and your supervisors have been notified to watch for him in your area. We've done everything we can to protect you, but I'm afraid that he got all your information when our files were hacked into."

Dillon grabbed the phone from her hand and began yelling into it.

Tracy jumped frantically off Dillon's lap and started running around the house gathering her things. She had to get away. If he found her, he would not only kill her, but he would kill everyone who knew her and anyone who helped her.

"Scott, are you safe?" she screamed as she grabbed the phone from Dillon.

"Yes, Tracy, things here are now secure, and we all have guards around the clock. Don't worry about anyone here," he patiently replied to her.

"Okay," she answered. She wanted to panic and run but knew that wasn't the smart thing to do. She needed more information, and the only person to get it from was Scott.

Dillon took the phone back from her, asking Scott how bad things were and what he recommended for Tracy to do.

While Dillon was talking to Scott, Tracy paced the room, biting her lip, trying to figure out what she should do now. She was sure Dillon would have some ideas when he got off the phone.

After several minutes of talking, Dillon set the phone down and motioned her to stand before him. He pulled her down onto his lap and just held her for several minutes.

Pulling slightly away from her, but not far enough that she missed him, he looked down at her. "Oh baby, we need to talk," he said before kissing her.

Settling her more comfortably in his lap, he relayed to her what he had learned from his conversation with Scott. He had been paroled but was not to leave the state of Utah, where Tracy lived before she was relocated by the witness protection program. He had been fitted with a tracking device that would not only notify his parole officer of his location at all times but also would sound an alarm if he left the state. He had been released for about a week when his parole officer disappeared. There was no trace of the woman, her credit cards hadn't been used, her bank account was untouched, and she was just gone.

"What we need to know from you, sweetie," he said, "is did he have any friends who would help him, anyone he could go to for money or a place to hide. Do you know of anyone like that?"

Tracy thought for a long time before answering Dillon. "He never introduced me to any of his friends or colleagues. I can try to reach the people who got us together. I haven't talked to them for several years, but they might still be in the same place."

"That would be good, but I don't want you contacting them. You would have to blow your cover. We don't want that. I will have someone from the Utah office visit them. Give me their info, and I'll take care of it. For now, we have to assume that he has your information and is either on his way here or is here already. You will stay here. I or another member of the team will be with you every minute of the day."

Tracy nodded her understanding. He would kill her if he found her. She couldn't spend the rest of her life hiding. Hopefully, they would catch him soon. She was back in the nightmare again.

Chapter Five

Dennis Crank spent six years in that fucking prison before his lawyer convinced the parole board to let him out. It was all that little bitch Carrie's fault. Only she wasn't Carrie anymore. Looking at the paper her information was on, he saw her name, Tracy. Tracy Smith was what she called herself now. She hadn't even kept his name. To him, she would always be Carrie Crank. Even though he hadn't married her, he had made her take his name. She was his, and he would get her back no matter what it took. Killing the bitch would be too easy. He just needed to be tougher with her. He hadn't been tough enough before. This time the slut would learn her lesson.

Dennis sat in his car outside the house he knew his Carrie was in. She was with that man, the man she had been with at the flea market. He should have killed Dwayne for walking up to her, but that was the only way they had been able to make sure it was really her. There had been so many mistakes before, he had to be sure that it really was her this time.

It wouldn't be long before she figured out that her phone and e-mail had been tapped, but that didn't matter now that he knew where she was. He just needed to be patient. She would be alone eventually, and then he could make his move.

After a week of watching the house, he still wasn't any closer to Carrie. He refused to call her Tracy. She would always be his Carrie. There was always someone with her. Either the asshole that apparently owned the house—his name was Dillon something according to the records Dwayne had found—or some other jerk. How many men was the whore sleeping with? He would just add that to her list of punishments. It was a long one after all the years she had been gone.

He planned on punishing her for every day he had spent in that prison and everything that happened to him while he was there. And the slut was going to pay for all the time and money he'd spent finding her ass too. Yes, this was going to be a fun punishment for him, but the cunt wouldn't enjoy it much.

It had been risky going by the old house to find some of his favorite toys, but he needed those to complete his plans. Dwayne secured them a house in a private area where he could take the bitch and have his fun. The only payment Dwayne asked was that he be included in the fun. What the bastard didn't know was that once his part was done and Dennis didn't need him anymore, he was disposable. Dwayne knew too much for Dennis to keep him alive.

Dwayne knew about the trail of bodies. Before they found Carrie, there had been other women Dwayne brought him, thinking it was her. Of course, after they saw him, he couldn't leave them alive. By the time he and Dwayne had finished with them, they didn't want to live anyway.

Now he needed to come up with a plan to get the bitch alone. He couldn't take her as long as she was with someone, and the cunt never seemed to be alone.

Tracy looked out the window again. She'd seen that car parked across the street before. It had been there off and on for days. Dillon said it was nothing to worry about, but it made her nervous.

At first, it had been one man, but now the man looked different, and the car had changed. Whoever it was just sat there for hours.

Link walked up behind her and pulled her away from the window. "Come on, honey, that's not doing any good," he told her as he pulled her over to the couch to sit.

Link Davis also worked for the Secret Service with Dillon, and he was staying with her today while Dillon was in court testifying on a case. Tracy knew Link well and had worked with him on several cases.

"Sit here, Tracy. You're like a caged animal. Dillon really needs to take you to the club for a good scene. Honey, even if he is out in that car, there's nothing you can do about it. When was the last time you and Dillon played?"

Link was also a part owner of the Mix and had been involved in the lifestyle for as long as Tracy could remember. He didn't have a permanent sub, but played often at the club and was a very popular Dom. When he settled down, a lot of hearts were going to be broken. Most nights he could be found at the club either playing or bartending.

"Dillon and I haven't played since this all started, Sir," Tracy answered him. Even though Link wasn't her Dom and she had never played with him, it was a submissive's duty to be respectful to all Doms.

"Well, I'm going to talk to him and see if we can't fix that. You're very tense, and he's not taking care of your needs right now."

Link knew Dillon was as upset as Tracy was about this. Dillon hadn't wanted to leave her, but without his testimony, there was no case, and the person on trial was too dangerous to let go.

Tracy got up to go to the window again, and Link pulled her down. "Stay here, sweetheart. Looking out there doesn't help anything." Link needed to find something to keep her occupied. "Tracy, go find some cards. We're going to play some poker." That would keep her busy for a while. He looked at his watch. Dillon was probably going to be gone another hour or two.

Tracy got the cards and set up a place for them to play at the table, bringing drinks for both of them. "So are we playing for money or what?" she asked after getting everything ready.

"Tracy, you know the rules. Doms and subs only play strip poker," Link told her. That would keep her away from the window for a while, and by the time he had her naked, Dillon should be home to deal with her.

"Oh, yes, Sir," she answered him, her tone of voice surly.

Link ignored her tone and dealt the cards. Tracy's mind was not on the game, and by the fourth hand, she was down to her underwear. She had just lost her fifth hand when Dillon walked in.

"Okay, honey, bra or thong, your choice," Link told her. He had her just where he wanted her. Time to hand her over to Dillon and let him finish the fun with her.

Handing the deck of cards to Dillon, Link headed for the door. "I'll see you two at the club later," he said as he walked out.

Dillon looked like he had been to hell and back. Tracy jumped up and ran to him, wrapping her arms around him and holding him close.

He had removed his tie and undone the first few buttons of his shirt in the car. Tracy slid her hand into his shirt over his heart, just holding it in place, trying to provide any comfort she could. Not saying a word, she took his hand and led him toward the bedroom, pulling him along behind her.

When they got to the bedroom, she pushed his suit jacket off his shoulders and pulled it from his arms before taking it and hanging it up. Then she did the same with his shirt, only laying it over the chair in the room before pushing him to sit on the bed. She knelt before him and reached for the belt on his pants, looking into his eyes before she started to release it.

Dillon smiled and nodded at her, giving her the permission she silently asked for.

Tracy slid his belt out of his pants and laid it on the bed beside him. Then she unfastened the button and zipper of his pants. He stood and let her remove them, then let her push him back onto the bed again.

Tracy knelt between his legs and took his cock with both hands. Lightly grasping him with her palms, she swept her hands up and down his hardening shaft. She leaned forward and touched her tongue to the very tip of his cock, tasting the drop of moisture that had formed there. Pulling her tongue back into her mouth, she sighed at the slightly sweet, slightly spicy taste that was Dillon.

He fisted his hands in her hair and pulled her to him, guiding her to take the head of his shaft in her mouth.

Tracy swirled her tongue around and around, gathering the droplets as they formed. Pulling back, she licked from the root to the tip, cupping and squeezing his balls as she did. Tracy took Dillon's dick in her mouth back as far as she could. She knew this was what he liked and wanted to please him. She had seen the pain in his face that reliving the nightmare today had caused him and knew this was comfort only she could give him.

With his hands in her hair, Dillon held Tracy's head still while he thrust in and out of her mouth, amazed at how deep she could take him. She was nowhere near the first woman to give him a blow job, but she was by far the best. Releasing his cum into her mouth, he lay back on the bed and allowed her to clean him up before pulling her to lie across him.

Unfastening her bra and pushing her thong down her legs, he told her, "Baby, you're wearing too many clothes." He let her sit up and remove the garments.

Tracy lay back on him, naked, and rubbed her nipples across his abrasive chest hair before laying her head on his shoulder, sprawling her naked body across his.

Dillon wrapped his arms around her and held her. The case today had been a bad one, and he was glad to have it over with. The suspect had been one heinous bastard, and Dillon had had nightmares for days after closing the case. Knowing that his testimony would help convict the ass would help, but the images it brought back would haunt him for weeks, again.

Tracy lay across his chest and let him hold her, feeling his breathing calm and the tension flow out of his body. Knowing it would help, she asked, "Can you tell me about it?" She had been involved in the case, but not the arrest, and knew this was a bad one. Dillon had been more involved than she was since he had been the one guarding the ass. Had he not interrupted when he did, the situation would have been much worse.

A couple of years back when Derek's wife, Dottie, had almost been kidnapped for a slave ring, they thought they had ended the kidnappings and caught one of the major players. Come to find out it was just one of the minors, and the kidnappings had continued. The president had continued relations with the country, hoping to get more information and stop the torture and kidnappings, but things continued to get worse. Now the asses were after a younger crowd, and the girl Dillon had rescued was only thirteen years old. He had never told Tracy the whole story, but she knew it had been bad. Derek and her supervisors had pulled her out due to her background, but she was involved long enough to know what was happening.

"Tell me what you can. It will help," she asked him again. She could tell he was hurting, and this was one of the ways she could help.

Dillon sighed and started rubbing his hand up and down her back, stopping occasionally to cup a breast or buttock. "Her parents were there with her. She looked like hell. Damn, if she weighed seventy pounds, it would have amazed me. When they put her on the stand to tell her story, all the ass did was yell, 'Diplomatic immunity! Diplomatic immunity!' The judge finally had to have him removed from the court. He smiled at the girl as he was taken out and said, 'I'll be back for you, sweetie,' grinning like a cat with the cream. Her mother broke out in hysterics at this, and if looks could have killed, everyone her father laid eyes on would have been dead. The attorney the scum retained kept trying to put the blame on the poor girl, and she just sat there sobbing through the entire trial, as did her mother and older sister. The sister kept crying, 'It should have been me.'"

Tracy snuggled closer to him, just letting him talk it all out. She knew how testifying at these things could be, and even though you were helping the victims, it still took a lot out of you, and the memories it brought back could haunt a person for months.

She placed soft kisses along his chest and nestled closer, giving him the warmth of her body and silently telling him it was going to be okay.

They lay for a long time, just talking and cuddling, until they both forgot their problems and drifted off to sleep, content to be together.

Chapter Six

It was dark by the time Dillon and Tracy woke. "Dress for the club, love," he told her. "I think we would both benefit from playing tonight, and I want to play with you."

Tracy nodded and went to figure out something to wear. While she was looking through her club clothes, Dillon asked her, "Do you want to try one of the theme rooms tonight? If you do, I'll call and have Link reserve one before they are all booked."

Tracy thought for a minute. She'd never played in the theme rooms but heard it was fun. When Dottie and Tammy had told her about the scenes they did with their men, it was very hot.

"You pick the room. It sounds like fun," she answered Dillon, finally settling on a hot-pink corset and matching see-through skirt for the evening. The skirt was full and flowing and reached to midcalf. She had strappy four-inch-heeled shoes to match. At the last minute, she grabbed a hot-pink thong to add to the outfit. Dillon didn't like her wearing them, but the skirt was very see-through, and she needed something else.

Dillon was sitting in a chair in the living room when she came out. He was wearing his black leather pants and an open leather vest to match. He looked good enough to eat. Crooking his finger, he indicated for her to come and stand between his spread legs. Again motioning with his finger, he indicated for her to twirl.

"Very pretty, pet, but what do you have under the skirt?"

"What do you think I'm wearing? A thong," she answered smartly.

"Oh love, you asked for it now." He smiled at her. "I think we'll work a little punishment into our play tonight." He rose and wrapped his arm around her waist, guiding her to the door. "You can leave the thong on for now. We'll fix it when we get to the club."

Dillon walked her to his truck and helped her in before driving them to the club. After he checked them in, he walked her to the bar where Link was working. He grabbed them each a water and took a key from Link. Then off to the costume room they went.

"Find a maid's outfit, and meet me in the kitchen room. Leave the thong on," he told her, leaving her to change. For the scene he was developing in his head, he didn't need to change, just needed a few stock items he knew would be in the kitchen. His little sub was in for a treat.

Tracy went through the costumes until she found the one he'd asked for. It was a French maid's outfit, a very short, frilly skirt and an apron top that tied in the back, leaving her back bare and her breasts barely covered. Slipping the top over her head, she adjusted the skirt and grabbed the six-inch stilettos that went with it.

Carefully walking down the hall to the kitchen, she found Dillon sitting at the table, holding a broken mug. "Ms. Smith, late again, I see. I think this is the third time this week, isn't it?" he asked, starting the scene as she walked in.

"Yes, Mr. Polk. I'm sorry, Sir. Please don't fire me," she pleaded, looking at the broken mug in his hands.

Dillon turned the mug in his hands a few times before looking up at her and asking, "I don't suppose you know anything about this, do you, Ms. Smith? Mrs. Brown, the cook, found it when she was taking out the trash yesterday."

"Oh, well, Sir, it slipped out of my hand when I was emptying the dishwasher, and I just threw it away. You can take it out of my salary," she answered, pouting.

"Ms. Smith, you know you are to report all breakage to me or, in my absence, Mrs. Brown, no matter how inconsequential it may seem to you."

"Yes, Sir," Tracy answered, bowing her head. Dropping to her knees before him, she kept her eyes on the floor and begged, "Please, Mr. Polk, don't fire me. I'll do anything, but I can't lose my job."

Dillon placed one finger thoughtfully on his chin and slanted his head slightly. "Anything, Ms. Smith?" he asked, his voice full of intrigue.

"Yes, Mr. Polk, anything. Please, please don't fire me." She let a tear run down her face. This was fun.

Dillon grinned at her and said, "Well then, Ms. Smith, let's start by seeing what you have on under that uniform." He stood, placing his hands on his hips, and looked her up and down. "Strip now!" he commanded.

"But...but..." Tracy stuttered, trying to stay in character and not laugh.

"Now, if you please, Ms. Smith," Dillon answered, his voice still in that deep, dark place.

"Yes, Sir," Tracy answered, her tone snarky. She carefully slid the short skirt down her legs and stepped out of it, untying the apron strings and slipping it over her head. Standing there in her thong and heels, she crossed her arms over her breasts, shivering with anticipation.

"Arms at your sides, please, Ms. Smith," he ordered as he walked around her, running one finger across her shoulder blades, then the back of his hand across one breast. He walked his fingers down her stomach to her mound before cupping her there. "Very nice, Ms. Smith," he told her, grinning. He reached around and slid one finger under her thong and between the cheeks of her ass. Letting the thong go to snap back in place, he slapped one ass cheek. "Very, very nice. Now we need to talk about the consequences of your actions."

"Yes, Sir," she answered, hanging her head.

"I believe I've counted four offenses here today, your tardiness, the breakage, your uniform violation, and the disrespectful tone of voice you've been using. Am I correct?"

"Uniform violation, what uniform violation?" she answered, eyes on the floor.

"I don't believe the thong was part of the uniform you were given, was it, Ms. Smith?" he asked, snapping the thong strap again.

"No, Sir. I just thought..." Tracy let her voice trail off.

"Didn't Mrs. Brown explain the rules on your first day, Ms. Smith?" he asked, snapping the thong again.

"Yes, Sir," she answered, keeping her eyes on the floor.

"Then I believe it's time for some discipline. Remove the thong, and bend over the table," he ordered.

Pulling the cart of items he had prepared earlier closer, he ran his hand down her back to steady her. "What are your safewords, Tracy?" he asked, reminding her she could use them if she needed.

"Purple and orange, Sir."

"When do you need to use them?"

"When I need to slow down or when I become overwhelmed, Sir," Tracy answered.

"Good girl," he told her, leaning down to kiss her deeply. "Have you ever used ginger root, Tracy?" he asked, reaching for a bowl under the towel covering up the things he planned on using on the cart.

"No, Sir, but I saw a sub with it once. Her Master put it on her clit. I thought she was going to go through the ceiling."

Tracy remembered the girl had tears streaming down her face, and she told Tracy afterward that it wasn't bad; it just burned like fire after a while. "It doesn't hurt you," the woman explained and got a fresh piece to show Tracy how it worked. "Put this in your mouth and suck on it for a minute, but don't chew. Just make sure to wash it off your hands after, and don't get it near your eyes, honey," "As part of your punishment, we will be using it tonight," Dillon told her, running his hands over her ass. He couldn't wait to spank it with the ginger in her. The spanking would make her clench her ass, which would deepen the effects of the ginger. She was in for another intense night.

"Okay, honey, first I want to show you a little trick I learned overseas." Dillon had been in the army and traveled all over the world before settling down in Washington with the Secret Service.

Helping her stand up, he sat in a chair and pulled her onto his lap, her back to his front. Reaching around, he started twisting and pulling her nipples, creating hard little peaks before he was done. Kissing her thoroughly one more time, he reached to the cart and lifted the towel enough to pull out two sets of bamboo chopsticks, which he had already prepared.

"These will work as nipple clamps for tonight. I can adjust the rubber bands as tight or as loose as I want them. Behave, and they will be looser. Get mouthy with me, and I tighten them," he told her.

Tracy looked at the chopsticks and ran her finger over the flat part of them, thinking they couldn't be much worse than clamps, and nodded. He had been planning this for a while, she could tell.

Dillon played with her nipples for a few more minutes, then applied the first set of chopsticks. It wasn't bad, Tracy thought, until he twisted the rubber band a few more times.

"Tight enough, baby?" he asked, watching her grimace.

"Fine, Sir," she answered smartly.

"Great." Dillon chuckled before tightening the band a couple more times for fun.

"Ugh," Tracy grunted, wishing she had kept her mouth shut.

He treated the other breast the same way, then laid her over the table again. The pressure of lying on her breasts tightened the chopsticks, and she moaned.

He ran his hands through her slit and found her dripping. "You're not enjoying this at all, are you?" he asked sarcastically, moistening her lips with her own juices.

Tracy moaned again, arching her back as he ran one finger around her clit and slipped two fingers inside her.

"Good girl," he praised her when he leaned over and bit the back of her neck.

Dillon lay over her for a minute before straightening up and grabbing the bowl of ginger he had prepared while waiting on her.

"This is small, baby, and I'm going to slip it inside you. I can't use any lube, or you won't get the full effects, and I want you to enjoy every moment as much as I will," he said with an evil grin.

He took the finger-sized piece of ginger and carefully slid it into her ass, rimming it around a few times.

"Now for your punishment. I'm going to give you twenty smacks before we move on, Ms. Smith. Hopefully, this will remind you to be more prompt in the future," he said as he started smacking her ass sharply with his hand. After the first ten smacks, he ran his hand down through her folds, making sure she was still where he wanted her.

"How are you doing, Tracy? Are you still good to go?" he asked her.

Tracy was starting to feel the effects of the ginger, and not only her ass was burning, but her clit was starting to get with the program too. "I'm good, Sir," she answered, unable to hold back the moan in her voice.

Dillon could see she was ramping up and knew he needed to keep things going. He didn't want her coming before he was ready for her too.

Grabbing a wooden spoon from the cart, he gave her the next ten smacks with it, making sure a couple struck on her little asshole, shoving the root a little deeper.

Finishing with the spoon, he grabbed a glove and pulled the ginger out, rimming it around a few times before removing it. It had been in long enough. Then he flipped her over onto her back and pulled her to the edge of the table so that her ass hung off the edge. He removed the chopsticks from her breasts and listened to the moan it caused. He moved the table chairs where he could prop her feet on them and spread her legs wide apart. He removed the leather vest and draped it over one of the chairs. Then he stepped between her legs and leaned over her and kissed her thoroughly, rubbing his chest over her still-sore nipples. He grinned. He rubbed his leather-covered crotch between her legs, cupping each breast and rubbing his thumbs over her throbbing nipples. Tracy moaned and arched her pelvis, needing more.

She was so close. All he needed to do was touch her clit, and she would come. Even though he had taken the ginger out of her ass, she could still feel the burn, and she felt it all the way to her pussy and clit.

Dillon stepped back and freed his raging hard-on from his leathers. If he didn't get himself in check, this would go much faster than he had planned. He continued rubbing her nipples before grabbing a plastic spatula from the table.

"Now for the next part of your punishment, Ms. Smith. I believe we've dealt with your tardiness for now. Let's talk about your clumsiness next." He took the spatula and tapped each nipple five times with it, watching her face to make sure he wasn't pushing her too much.

Tracy moaned and arched, her nipples still sensitive from the clamps he had used earlier.

"Do you think you will remember this punishment next time you try to hide something from me?" he asked her, leaning down and biting each nipple.

"Yes, Sir," Tracy answered, panting. She wasn't sure how much more she could take. "Permission to come, Sir."

"Not until your punishment is over, Ms. Smith," Dillon answered her, his tone of voice steely.

"Ugh, hurry it up then," Tracy groaned, unable to help herself.

Dillon put down the spatula and took a small spoon from the still-cloth-covered cart and stepped back between her legs. Squatting down so that his face was level with her pussy, he took her clit in his mouth and sucked it hard.

Tracy arched and moaned again. "Please, Sir. Permission to come," she begged.

"Soon, baby, soon," Dillon answered her, pulling at her clit with his teeth.

Tracy moaned again and bit her lip hard. She had been in the lifestyle for several years, and Dillon often made her hold her orgasms back, but she wasn't going to be able to last much longer if he didn't give her some relief soon.

Dillon took the spoon and held it over her clit, pulling it back with one finger to let it flick the little nub.

"Oh my God," Tracy moaned, "no fair." She arched her pelvis again. She had almost come with that one, and if he did it again, she didn't know what she'd do.

Biting her lip hard enough to almost draw blood, Tracy pulled herself back from the edge one more time.

Dillon could see the struggle she was having, and even though this was a punishment session, he didn't want her feeling like a failure, so with the next flick of the spoon, he added the command "Come" and sat back to watch her fall apart.

Tracy screamed Dillon's name as the world around her split into pieces. All of her limbs felt as if separated from her body, and she didn't think she'd ever be able to move again. Just as she was starting to come back together again, Dillon flicked the spoon onto her clit again, setting her off one more time. Her voice hoarse from screaming, all she could do was rasp his name over and over again between panting breaths.

Dillon gave her a little more time to gather herself together this time before covering his rigid cock with a condom. Adding lube to the condom and applying some to her little hole, he lifted her knees over his shoulders and slowly slid his hard cock into her little ass. He knew she would still be tingly and tender from the ginger, but he couldn't wait any longer.

Tracy barely had the strength to moan when Dillon slid his cock into her ass, but felt her body tuning up again. She didn't know if she could handle another one. Was it possible to die from orgasm overload? She guessed she'd find out, because it didn't look like Dillon was ready to stop anytime soon.

Chapter Seven

After Dillon was finished with Tracy in the kitchen theme room, he called Link to have the room cleaned and carried his girl to one of the suites he had reserved earlier. He laid Tracy on the bed while he ran a hot bath for her, then carried her into the tub. After gently washing her, he sat holding her on his lap, soothing her body with his hands, until the water cooled. He carefully dried her and wrapped her in a fluffy towel. Then he dried himself before carrying her to bed. Laying her in the center, he removed the towel and crawled in behind her. She snuggled her bottom to his pelvis and went immediately to sleep. Dillon lay awake holding her for the longest time, thinking and planning.

He had to figure out how to lure that asshat Dennis out of hiding so he and Tracy could go on with their lives. Tracy was going nuts being cooped up in the house, but it wasn't safe to let her out. He had talked to Derek and Tyler about it, and they all agreed it wasn't safe for Tracy to be anywhere near her friends until Dennis was caught. He might try to use her friends to get to her. They didn't know how unstable he was and what he was capable of. He had been overheard in the jail making threats about her, but nothing had been reported until after his parole, and then it was too late.

When Dillon found out whose lame idea it was to release him from prison, he would make sure the ass was fired and never worked in the justice field again. Talk about a cluster fuck. This was one of epic proportions.

He was glad he had been able to get Tracy out of her head for a while tonight. He had seen the tension radiating off her in waves for the past few days, but hadn't been able to bring her to the club until tonight. Derek had limited the people in the club tonight and had brought in extra security so that Dillon could safely bring Tracy. He and Tracy would be on permanent babysitting duty with Micah, Derek's young son, for a while after this. That was if he could get her to agree to stay with him and marry.

He had never been one of those guys who yearned for a family and normal life, but after meeting Tracy and seeing how happy his friends were, he longed for that now. He had both Derek and Tyler looking for property close to their house for him to buy and hoped he could talk Tracy into selling her house. He wanted a future and children with her.

She squirmed in his arms and moaned a little. He looked down at her face. She was still sleeping, maybe dreaming. He kissed the top of her head and pulled her closer, tucking the covers around them, mingling his legs with hers.

Chapter Eight

Tracy paced the length of the living room again, trying to avoid looking out the window. She had pulled a chair over to the window once, planning on sitting there and staring out. Eventually, Dennis or whoever was in the car would show himself, and then she would know for sure. Patrol officers had been to the car several times and had made them move, but since they weren't doing anything illegal, there wasn't much that could be done. Dillon offered to pull whoever it was out of the car and beat the shit out of them until they said why they were there, but as good an idea as Tracy thought that was, it really wasn't. Dillon could go to jail, or worse, the ass could hurt him. The patrol officers had checked identification, and it wasn't Dennis. One had even snapped a picture with his cell phone and brought the picture to Tracy just in case the jerk was using a fake ID. No, she confirmed, not Dennis.

There had been several different cars, all rentals, over the past couple of weeks, none for more than two or three days, but always in the same place, and as far as anyone could tell, always with the same driver. Since the night Dillon took Tracy to the club, they hadn't been out of the house except for short trips to the office or to the store. Other than that they were both working on reports from home and catching up on paper work. Tracy was about to go batshit crazy. Something had to break soon.

That night Dillon took Tracy to bed early. He wanted to play. They both needed it. The scene was short but intense and just what they both needed. Tracy fell, exhausted and sated, to sleep in his arms for the first time in days.

They were both sound asleep when the house phone rang, and the alarms on both their cell phones rang. Tyler had set the alarm system on Tracy's house to notify both of them, the police, and fire department if anything should happen. This was the fire notification. There was a fire somewhere in Tracy's house.

Throwing on clothes, they both ran to Dillon's truck and quickly drove to Tracy's house. Neither of them noticed that the rental car that was usually parked across the street was absent, in their hurry to find out what was going on.

Dillon drove as quickly and as safely as possible to Tracy's, trying to assure her on the way that everything would be okay. By the time they got to the house, the police and fire departments had already arrived, and several of Tracy's neighbors were standing in the street, making it difficult to get through. Finally leaving his truck in the middle of the street, Dillon and Tracy jumped out and ran to the house. After providing identification, the firefighters let her and Dillon into the house. The blaze had been small and contained to one room, so the damage was mostly smoke and water.

As one of the firefighters was escorting them to the room where the fire started, a police officer came into the house and called for Dillon. "Sir, you are going to have to move your truck. If you follow me, I'll escort you to an area we've set up for parking," he said as he walked Dillon out of the house to his truck.

Looking back over his shoulder, Dillon didn't want to leave Tracy but knew she wouldn't come with him and that she wanted to see what had happened and how much damage there was.

The firefighter was very nice and helped Tracy over the debris as he led her to her bedroom, where the fire had started. As they were walking up the stairs, another officer came into the house.

"Ms. Smith," he called, "I need you to come with me. We found something we want you to see." He took her arm and guided her out the door. Holding her arm tightly, he pulled her to a black sedan and, opening the back door, shoved her in.

Chapter Nine

Dillon finally got his truck moved and ran back to Tracy's house. Calling for her, there was no answer. The firefighter that let them into the house answered to check with the police. She had gone with one of them over paper work or something.

Dillon ran outside and looked at the groups of people congregating there and didn't see Tracy.

Walking up to the first officer he saw, he asked about Tracy. The man knew nothing but quickly sent out a radio broadcast, asking for all officers to check in, and then called his captain to inform him of the situation. Dillon was starting to get a very bad feeling. This was not good. He quickly called Derek, Link, and Tyler, saying three words, "FUBAR. Tracy's. Now!" before hanging up.

He didn't wait for the police to act or his friends to arrive and started checking with each group of spectators, asking if they had seen Tracy. After asking several people, one group finally remembered seeing a policeman shove her into the back of a car, and then the car took off. Calling one of the policemen over to the group to hear the story, he made a conference call to his friends and told them it looked like the ass may have gotten to Tracy. Running his hands through his hair, he tried to calm his racing heart and formulate a plan.

They had no idea where the ass could have taken her, but he was sure he knew what the bastard was going to do to her. The longer she was with him the more she would be hurt.

Tracy woke lying on the floor in a strange room. She had a ball gag in her mouth so big that it hurt her jaw. Her mind was fuzzy. Where was she? How had she gotten there? What was going on? Trying to focus her eyes, she looked around. Why was everything so blurry, and why did she hurt so bad? Had she been drugged? Why couldn't she focus?

"Awake are you, slut?" a strange voice asked.

Turning her head to the side, she looked for the source of the voice. Just the small movement made the room spin again, and she knew then any big movement would be worse.

She tried to push herself into a sitting position, only to find she was tied down. Moving slowly she tested each limb, no movement. She was fastened tight.

"Just hang on, bitch. Dennis will be here soon. Then the fun will start," the voice said again, and something pinched one of her nipples. Hard.

Dwayne rubbed his hands together and wiped the drool from his face. It was all he could do to keep from fucking the whore right now. Where the hell was Dennis, and why had he agreed to wait? Looking at the array of floggers, whips, crops, canes, and other torture implements laid out on the table, he tried to decide what he wanted to use first on the cunt.

Where the hell was Dennis anyway, he asked himself again. He had texted him right after he got the slut in the car and drugged. He should be here by now.

Pacing back and forth, he couldn't resist torturing the slut every time he walked past her—slapping her tits, grabbing her crotch—thinking about all the things he could and would do to her. Grabbing his phone, he sent a text again to Dennis. He had promised he wouldn't do anything to the slut until Dennis got there, but the fucker better hurry.

The one person that had seen Tracy shoved into the car didn't have many details, but the description she gave of the man didn't match Dennis. The license plate came back as a rental car, and the rental company listed the person who had leased it as Dwayne Woods.

Dillon ran to his truck and grabbed his laptop, hoping to work his magic. Setting up programs to track everything Dwayne Woods had done in the past month was too easy for the computer genius. All he could do now was wait and see what he could find. If the man farted in the wrong place, Dillon would find out.

Derek, Link, and Tyler arrived and started canvassing the remaining witnesses, leaving Dillon to his computer.

Dillon managed to find a picture of Dwayne for the guys and police to show around, and soon he had confirmation that the man who had shoved Tracy into the car was him and he had been the man sitting outside the house for the past few weeks.

Now to figure out where the ass could have taken Tracy and what his connection to Dennis Crank was. Dillon typed furiously on his laptop, doing traces and setting traps, everything he could think of to find his woman.

After the guys talked to every one of Tracy's neighbors and all of the spectators at the fire twice, they checked in with Dillon to see if he had found out anything more and how he was doing.

Dillon had been sitting in his truck working on his laptop, not wanting to leave the area in case Tracy was still somewhere close. Derek convinced him to go home. His computer there would be faster, and he would get better results than he would on his laptop. Link promised to stay and watch Tracy's house in case she would return. He really did have good friends.

When Dillon got home, Tyler was sitting on his porch waiting. "What are you doing here?" he asked.

"I pulled the short straw and got stuck babysitting you. It's my job to make sure you don't go off half cocked and do something stupid," Tyler answered.

"Isn't Tammy about to pop? She'll kick your ass if you're not there."

"She's got another month or so—and if you tell anyone this, your ass will be the one kicked—but she's driving me nuts, and I could use a break. I love her with all my heart, but she's miserable and cranky, and I can't do anything right. I'm tired of her throwing things at me. Just as soon as I can, I'm going to redden that ass so bad she won't sit for a month," Tyler joked, trying to get a smile out of Dillon. He hated seeing his friend sad and wished there was more he could do.

Once in the house, Tyler went to make coffee, and Dillon headed for his computer. Maybe the searches he had started on the laptop had found something.

Opening the programs, one by one, to no results, he was starting to get frustrated before he opened the last one, the one he had set up to search for vacation rentals. He screamed at the top of his lungs and ran for Tyler. "He rented a cabin, a fucking cabin! Grab your phone. Start calling, ambulance, cops, Derek—fuck, call out the army. I want it all converging on this location," He ran for his guns and his truck. The asshole was caught now.

Dillon drove frantically to the remote location where the cabin was located, and Tyler managed to calm him down somewhat on the way. "Man, we need to have a plan. We can't just go rushing in, or Tracy could get caught in the middle. Think this out," he told him.

Dillon knew Tyler was right, but all he could think of was getting to Tracy and kicking the shit out of the ass that had taken her. When he was done with that ass, her ex was next.

"Man, you're right, but I can't think of anything but getting to her right now. You and Derek plan it out, and I'll go along with it." He hoped he could follow a plan. All he wanted right that moment was Tracy safe in his arms.

The cabin they thought Tracy was in was located about a half mile off the road, in a quiet, isolated part of the woods. It would be hard to sneak up on it. They would have to go in on foot and leave the vehicles behind, carrying what they could.

Derek and Link met them on the way to the cabin, and they split up to come at it from different directions. As they walked up, Dillon knew something was wrong. It was too quiet and too easy.

"She's not here. They set a fucking trap. Back to the truck," he screamed, and they all took off running just before the cabin blew into a thousand pieces.

When they got to the truck, they all leaned against it, panting. "How did you know she wasn't there?" Derek asked.

"Instinct," Dillon answered. If she had been there, he would have felt it. The asses had set a fucking trap. Now he had to start all over.

"What now?" Tyler asked.

"Back to the fucking start. I should have known it was too easy," Dillon answered. He had to dig deeper.

They drove quietly back to Dillon's house, and Dillon thought of what else he could do. Digging deeper into Dennis and Dwayne's histories, he set up traces on the parents and family of both men, looking for unusual activity on all of the names he could find. They had to have her close. He doubted Crank would have the patience to wait to get to her.

Chapter Ten

Dwayne couldn't believe it when Dillon called and told him they had to move the bitch to the second location, that the feds were on the way. Throwing the black hood over the slut's face, he undid the chains holding her down and threw her over his shoulder, carrying her to the van and throwing her in. Lucky for him, she was still out of it from the drugs he had given her, and she didn't fight him. He had dumped the car in town and traded it for the van his cousin had rented for them. That was one cousin that would never bother him again.

He was glad Dennis had thought all this up. He would have never been able to do it on his own. Dwayne wasn't stupid, but he wasn't winning any genius awards either. The only thing he had going for him was his looks. He was a fairly attractive man and didn't have any trouble finding women, but they didn't last long after he started his games with them. Women were just too fragile for what he needed. "Sadist" was too mild of a word to use to describe his tastes.

Tracy grunted when her back hit the floor of the van. She knew if she was going to escape, she had to do it soon. Once they got wherever they were going was too late. She wished her head didn't hurt so bad. It was hard to think. She had to get away.

It was dark in the back of the van. There were no windows, and the only light was what came from the instrument panel in the front. They must be in the country. There were no streetlights and no other cars. Even if she did manage to get out of the van, there was little chance of help, and if she had to run and hide in the woods, naked, her skin would be ripped to shreds by the foliage and tree branches. She had to think. There must be something she was missing.

Maybe she could use her nakedness to her advantage. She made herself cough several times, and started crying, "I'm so cold," hoping he wouldn't gag her again. He had made the mistake of leaving her arms and legs free. A well-placed knee or elbow would disable him. She just had to get him close enough to take down.

Coughing again, she let her voice go hoarse and pleaded, "A blanket, please. I'll do anything you want."

"Shut the fuck up, bitch." Dwayne answered her plea, remembering that Dennis had told him to be careful around her. But what the hell could one bitch do to him?

The cabin he had gotten his cousin to rent wasn't that far from the first, and it didn't take long for Dwayne to pull onto the deserted-looking road. The reason they had picked this for their second location was because it was so well hidden. No one was going to find them there.

Tracy pulled herself into a ball, hoping in the dark to get the advantage on Dwayne. It was the only choice she had. Even though he was a lot bigger than her, if she timed it right and had the advantage of surprise, she might be able to use his size against him.

It wasn't much longer before Dwayne pulled the van to a stop and got out, leaving Tracy alone in the blackness of the van.

Moving around and positioning herself in front of the side door, Tracy prepared herself for a fight.

As Dwayne opened the side door of the van, Tracy attacked. Screaming at the top of her lungs, she slammed the heel of her hand into his nose and her foot into his crotch, knocking him backward out of the van. Following him out and onto the ground, she applied sharp elbows and knees to soft places until he had him immobilized.

With Dwayne passed out on the ground, Tracy had to figure out her next move. She had to assume Dennis was either on his way or somewhere close.

Being as quiet as she could, she looked into the windows of the cabin. The lights were on, but she didn't see anyone, and the only vehicle around was the van Dwayne had brought her in. She was sure Dennis wouldn't be walking from the main road to the cabin. Now she just needed a place to hide until she could figure out what to do next.

"Damn it all to hell. I thought we had the fuckers," Dillon stormed. He was pissed as all hell. He had to find Tracy and do it quick. Lord only knew what they were doing to her. It was all his fault for leaving her. If he ever got her back, he was going to handcuff her to him and never let her out of his sight again.

"Man, I'm not going to tell you to calm down, but you need to. You're the computer genius. Think, man. What else can you do?" Derek could always make him see reason when no one else could.

None of his programs had found anything. That meant he needed to dig deeper. He extended his search to cousins and coworkers of Dwayne and Dennis, knowing if he didn't get results with this search, Tracy could be out of time.

Dillon had the computers tracing all the activity on Dwayne's family's credit cards. Hearing a ping that meant the computer had found something, he ran to the screen to see what he had found.

"Well," he announced to the group, "Dwayne's cousin rented a black cargo van two days ago. We can assume that's what they are driving. I'll send the info to all the cops to be on the watch for it."

Pacing the room back and forth, Dillon finally grabbed his coat and keys. "Where are you going?" Tyler asked.

"They can't have taken her that far. I'm going to check out all the roads and cabins close to where we lost them at. She has to be close. Link can watch the computers," Dillon answered.

"I'm going with you. If you find her, you're going to need someone to drive while you take care of her," Derek answered, grabbing blankets and a first aid kit.

Dillon knew better than to argue and just headed for his truck. Time to find his girl.

Dennis couldn't believe his eyes when the bitch took Dwayne down. How the crazy fuck let the slut get the jump on him, he had no idea. Now he had her all to himself. This might be better than the original plan. Dennis was always a man who prided himself on thinking on his feet. It was what had kept him alive in the world.

Watching the bitch sneak around the cabin and look in the windows, it was all Dennis could do to keep from jumping her. He wanted to let her get in the cabin. Then he would have her trapped.

Tracy looked around the outside of the cabin trying to find something she could use as a weapon. She may have been lucky enough to get the jump on Dwayne but wasn't counting on being able to get that lucky with Dennis.

After looking in all the windows and convincing herself the cabin was empty, Tracy crept up onto the porch and turned the doorknob. Surprised when it opened under her fingers, she let herself in. The first thing she did was look for something to cover herself with and then a place to hide. The cabin was one big open room with no closets. The room was minimally furnished, and Tracy didn't see anything she could use as a weapon, but at least she was in out of the weather, and she had found an old torn and patched quilt to cover herself with. Now all she had to do was hope Dillon was on his way.

Dennis watched the bitch go into the cabin and knew he had her. Walking over to where Dwayne lay on the ground, he kicked him hard in the ribs before dragging him into the woods. He didn't want Dwayne coming to and interrupting his time with Tracy. Dennis walked around the outside of the cabin, making sure there was no way the slut could get out any of the windows and that the back door was blocked.

Grabbing his toy bag from where he had stashed it, he opened the door and walked into the cabin, announcing, "Hey, baby, Daddy's home," in a singsong voice.

Tracy stood in the middle of the cabin looking around. There was nothing, nowhere to hide, nothing to use as a weapon. "Dennis, think before you..." she started, trying to think of something to say to calm him down.

Dennis stalked over to Tracy and put a hand on each of her shoulders, pulling her toward him. Sliding his hands down her back, he nuzzled her hair and pulled her close. "I've missed you so bad, baby."

Dennis led Tracy over to the couch in the center of the room, in front of the fireplace. "Oh, Carrie baby, you're so cold. Let me start a fire and warm you up. Look at you out here all alone, no clothes, just waiting for your Master. You've been such a bad girl." He turned and sat her on the sofa, slapping her ass as he sat her down. "Now you stay put while your Master makes a fire."

Dennis was acting as if nothing had happened between them, and Tracy couldn't figure out his mood. She didn't know whether to play into the way he was acting or to try to run.

"Yes, Master," Tracy answered him in a quiet voice, trying to decide what to do. Where was Dillon? *Please be on your way,* she prayed.

Tracy looked and saw Dennis squatting in front of the fire and couldn't stop herself. Before she knew what she was doing, she had planted one foot in his ass and knocked him into the fire. Jumping up, she ran for the door. Not sure what to do next, she ran for the van as she heard Dennis screaming.

Halfway to the van, she saw Dillon. *Thank God!*

Launching herself at him, she barely noticed Derek running for the cabin and the screaming man inside. As Derek stepped on the porch, a loud explosion was heard, and he was knocked flat on his back on the ground. Dillon fell forward, landing on Tracy and also protecting her from the fallout of the explosion.

Chapter Eleven

The explosion in the cabin killed Dennis and started a huge fire in the woods. After it was all done, the fire department found a body in the trees, which they identified from dental records as Dwayne Woods, Dennis's old college roommate.

As Dillon and Derek backtracked Dennis and Dwayne's activities, they found that they had been the ones harassing Tracy. Tracy recognized Dwayne as the man from the flea market, and everything began to fit together.

Tracy wasn't hurt, but Dillon made her go to the hospital anyway to be checked out.

Derek ended up with some strained muscles in his back, but nothing that wouldn't heal with time.

After Tracy was released from the hospital, Dillon took her back to his house. Though the damage to her house from the fire was minimal, there was cleanup that needed to be done and a few repairs to be made.

Tracy was cold and distant with Dillon, and he couldn't figure out why. At first, he thought it was because of what she had been through and the memories it brought back, but after a few days, he realized there was more to it. Dillon tried to give Tracy space and time to heal, but she just became more closed off, until one day he came home to find her packing her things into her car.

"Where are you going, baby?" he asked, taking the box from her hands and putting it in the trunk of her car.

"My house is finished. There's no point in me and Tickles staying here any longer. I want to go home. I've imposed on you long enough," Tracy answered him. The last thing she wanted to do was go home to her house and be alone again, but things with Dillon were uncomfortable, and it was time for her to leave.

Since the night Dennis had been killed, things had been different. He was very gentle with her and didn't make demands. Something was missing. Tracy wanted more. She needed the Dom/sub relationship she thought they had been working toward before everything started with Dennis, and now Dillon acted like he didn't want that anymore. He still held her in his arms every night and made love to her often, but he hadn't tried to play with her and didn't talk about going to the club. When she acted bratty and tried to get in trouble, he just patted her and smiled at her.

She had done everything she could think of trying to pull him out of the funk he seemed to be in, but nothing helped. Finally tired of being unhappy with him, she decided to go home and be unhappy without him.

Tracy had hoped to be packed and out of the house before Dillon came back from running his errands, but that didn't happen. Now she was forced to face him.

Dillon stood by her car, hands in his pockets. He wanted to grab her and carry her into the house, where he would tie her to the bed and flog her until she saw reason, then fuck her into next week, but he knew he couldn't do that.

He had felt the distance between them growing with every day but didn't know what to do about it. The Dom in him told him to just tell her what was going to happen and be done with it, but he was scared of hurting her again. He knew from what she had told him about her past the terrible memories Dennis had brought back, and wanted to give her time to heal and get over that, but wasn't sure he was going about it the right way. Now he'd lost her.

Dragging her feet, Tracy grabbed her purse and the cat carrier from beside the door and walked to her car. Putting her things on the passenger seat, she turned and hugged Dillon. "Thanks for letting me stay," she said, kissing him softly on the mouth, wanting him to grab her and hold her tight, willing him to take the kiss over and dominate her. It didn't happen.

Tracy smiled and waved as she backed down the drive to the street, hoping Dillon couldn't see the single tear sliding down her cheek. She waited until she was at the end of the block before she really started crying.

Dillon walked slowly into the house. She'd been gone only a few minutes, and already the house was too big and lonely for him. Every part of him said he should get in his truck and chase her, that he shouldn't let her go, but he didn't. Grabbing a beer from the fridge, he started to sit on the couch, but kept remembering the night he had stripped her naked and tied her to the legs of it, then made her come until she was hoarse from screaming. Sitting in the chair was just as bad. If he kept his up, he would have to get rid of everything in the house. Hell, he might as well move. He'd taken her in every room and on every piece of furniture. Fuck, he'd have to sell his truck too.

Dumping the remainder of the beer down the drain, he threw the bottle in the trash and grabbed his keys, locking the door as he walked out of his house. Not knowing where else to go, he drove to the club. Link would be there, and maybe he could help him figure out what to do. He had fucked up.

When he got to the Mix, Derek and Tyler were sitting and talking to Link. Walking up to them, he grabbed a barstool beside Derek and asked what the two married men were doing hanging out at the club. Since they had gotten married, Derek and Tyler didn't go far without their wives, and it was unusual to see them in the club.

"The hens got together to talk baby stuff, and we were excused," Derek answered with a touch of sarcasm.

"More like dismissed," Tyler put in, resting his chin in his hands. "I can't wait for this baby to come. You should have warned me, you bastard," he said, punching Derek in the arm.

"Hell man, you had her married and pregnant before I had a chance," Derek answered, punching him back. Looking at Dillon he asked, "Where's Tracy?" Seeing the dejected look on his friend's face, he knew something was up.

"She left me. Packed up her stuff and the damned cat and went home," Dillon answered after asking Link for a shot of tequila. He needed something to numb the pain.

"And you let her, you fucker," Tyler answered. "That woman was the best thing that ever happened to you, you little asshole. You better not have hurt her, or I'll bust your jaw right here."

Dillon downed his shot and held the glass out for Link to refill. He might as well get drunk on his ass. Nothing else was going to happen, and he knew that Derek or one of the other guys would make sure he made it home safe.

After several more shots, Dillon couldn't stand hearing the sounds of the club anymore. Hands slapping skin, the sound of a flogger thudding on bare flesh, the screams of women and men coming, the smell of sex, it was all too much. Everything reminded him of Tracy. Lurching to his feet, he stumbled in the direction of the door.

Derek grabbed his arm just in time to keep him from falling over a sub crawling along behind her Master. "Where do you think you're going?"

"To get my woman. Who the hell does she think she is? She can't just up and leave me. I was going to marry her. I love her," Dillon slurred, sitting on his ass in the middle of the floor.

Derek looked to Tyler, and the two men hauled Dillon to his feet and led him out to Derek's truck. Since the women were at Derek's house, he had driven, which worked out well. Tyler could drive Dillon's truck home.

Getting Dillon into Derek's truck was a feat. He kept pulling away and trying to get to his truck. "I have to drive to Tracy's," he slurred. "I have to tell her she's marrying me." He started yelling for her. "Tracy, baby, I'm coming, baby."

Derek and Tyler finally got Dillon stuffed into Derek's truck, but it took a while. Derek finally had to agree to take Dillon to Tracy's. Derek wasn't really worried about it. He was pretty sure Dillon would pass out before they got anywhere near Tracy's, and called Dottie to have her make up the spare room. It looked as if they were going to have a house guest for the night.

Dillon rose from where he had slumped against the seat about halfway to Derek's house. "Where the fuck are we?" he asked.

"Taking you home, buddy. You're hosed, time to hang it up for the night." Derek chuckled

"No! I have to go talk to Tracy." Dillon was drunk, but not so drunk that he didn't know what he needed to do. He needed to get his woman—now!

"No, buddy, Dottie's making up the spare. You need to sleep this off before you do something you'll regret." Derek tried to reason with him, even though he knew better than to try to reason with a drunk.

"No, got to go see Tracy," Dillon mumbled, reaching for the door handle. He'd just get out and walk if Derek wouldn't take him.

"Hold on, buddy. I'll take you to see her," Derek told him, trying to calm him down. Knowing he could be making a big mistake, he turned the truck toward Tracy's. It was Dillon's mistake to make, not his, and he knew how he'd feel if Dottie left him. They needed to talk it out.

Derek pulled up in front of Tracy's house and walked Dillon to the door. "You sure you want to do this, buddy?" he asked, still not sure it was a good idea.

Dillon broke away from him and started pounding on Tracy's door and yelling her name.

Tracy opened the door wearing her softest, oldest robe, her hair was a mess, and she looked like she'd been crying. She was also holding a quart of ice cream, chocolate.

Dillon almost fell through the door, but Derek caught him. "He's had a few to drink but wanted to talk to you," he told Tracy with an apologetic smile on his face.

"No shit. You thought this was a good idea?" She glared accusingly at Derek, moving out of the way so he could bring Dillon into the house. "Put him on the couch. I'll take care of him," Tracy said, rolling her eyes. She couldn't believe she was letting Dillon in her house.

Derek helped Dillon in and then stood at the end of the couch, arms crossed against his chest. "He loves you, you know, and you hurt him."

"It didn't do me any good either," Tracy answered back, running her hand through her hair and helping put Dillon's legs up on the couch while avoiding his waving arms reaching out for her. Dillon was thrashing about so much Tracy was afraid he was going to fall off the couch. She looked at Derek and shook her head. "Here, help me get him back to the bed. He's never going to fit out here, and I can't pick him up off the floor."

Derek helped Tracy get Dillon to bed. Then she grabbed a tank top and pair of sweats, changing swiftly. She walked out to the porch, where Tyler was waiting with Derek.

"Tracy, you really fucked him up. You gonna take care of this?" Tyler asked, arms crossed over his chest. He and Derek stood side by side and looked every bit the Doms they were.

"You don't need to pull this shit on me. I know I hurt him. I hurt too. We need to talk to each other, but you guys don't know what's going on. He's changed. He doesn't want me anymore," Tracy managed to get out before she started crying again.

Derek relaxed and pulled her against his big body. At six foot eight inches and three hundred pounds, he was a mountain of a man but was a big teddy bear under all his gruffness. Tyler patted her on the back, and they all sat on her porch to talk.

"Honey, you need to talk to him. He doesn't understand why you left, and he thinks you don't want him or the lifestyle anymore," Tyler told her quietly.

While they all sat drinking at the club, Dillon had confessed his thoughts and fears to Derek, Tyler, and Link. He was just as confused as Tracy was.

"He is?" Tracy asked. She had been sure Dillon didn't want her anymore. Maybe she had just been misreading his signs. "If he wants me so bad, why won't he play with me? He won't take me to the club and doesn't even spank me for being bratty."

"Tracy," Derek started, taking a deep breath. He knew he shouldn't interfere, but damn it, Dillon and Tracy belonged together. Dottie, his wife, would kick his ass if he didn't do something. "Dillon's afraid of hurting you. He knows what Dennis put you through and is afraid that this incident brought back all those memories. He doesn't want you to think he's like Dennis and that all he wants is to beat you and have sex. He wants more with you. He's just afraid to ask for it, and I think you have been too. Both of you need to be honest with each other." When had he become a fucking counselor? "When he sobers up, talk to him, tell him what you want, how you feel, what you need from him, and don't take any of his bullshit." Derek took her in his arms and hugged her, standing her up and pushing her toward the house. "If he gives you any trouble tomorrow, call me. Here are the keys to his truck. Hide them until morning," Derek said as he grabbed Tyler by the arm and walked him away from the house. He had done his best with both of them, and now they needed to work it out.

Tracy locked her doors and turned the lights out, working her way back to the bedroom. What was she going to do? She stood at the side of the bed, looking down at Dillon passed out, for several minutes. He looked so peaceful asleep. She could picture his stern face when he was dominating her, his concerned look when she had told him about Dennis, his harshness when she disobeyed, the way his eyes lit up with laughter, the passion when he was inside of her. Could she give up all of him and what he did to and for her? Did she want to? Turning off the bedroom light, she lay down beside him and allowed her body to fit to his. As she snuggled down, getting comfortable, Dillon wrapped one arm and one leg over her, pulling her closer and nuzzling her neck in his sleep. She heard his soft sigh and felt his body relax as she did the same. Just like Scarlett in *Gone with the Wind*, she'd think about it tomorrow.

Tracy woke the next morning to find Dillon sitting on the side of the bed, head in his hands. Sitting up and maneuvering herself to sit beside him, she rubbed his back. He turned his head to look at her.

"So, tell me, how big of an ass was I?" he asked as if it hurt to talk.

"You were pretty passed out by the time Derek got you here. He helped me get you to bed, and you were out for the count. I'm going to make some coffee. You feel up to trying something to eat?" she asked, walking to the door.

"Maybe a case of aspirin. Do you mind if I hit the shower? I want to wash some of this disgust off," he said as he started stripping in preparation for his shower.

"Help yourself. You know where everything is. I'll go start some coffee and maybe some bacon and eggs."

"Yeah, sounds good," Dillon answered, hoping he felt semi-human after his shower. He couldn't believe how much he had drunk the night before. He hadn't done anything like that since he left the army. Now he remembered why.

Quickly showering, he put his jeans back on and walked out to the kitchen shirtless, rubbing a towel over his wet head. Draping the towel around his neck, he walked up behind Tracy and put his arms around her. "Finish that up. Then we need to talk," he told her, looking at the breakfast she was cooking.

Tracy finished the eggs she was cooking and took the plates to the table. "Sit. Eat. Then we'll talk." She put a plate in front of Dillon. She turned and grabbed the coffeepot, filling his cup with coffee before putting tea in her own.

Wrapping both her hands around her mug of tea, she looked down in the cup, hoping it would have the answers she had been looking for. They finished their breakfast in silence. Then Dillon helped her clean up. Finally, everything was done, and there were no more excuses.

Dillon took her by the hand and led her to the couch. Tracy wished she had taken the time to get dressed, feeling like she needed a suit of armor for protection. She felt too vulnerable in her tank and sweats.

Dillon sat next to her on the middle of the couch. Taking both her hands with his, he turned to look into her eyes. "Honesty, no lies, right?" he said, and she nodded. "Tell me what you want. Do you want me to leave you alone? Are we done?" he asked her, staring into her eyes, looking into her soul.

Tracy felt her eyes fill with tears. *No!* she screamed silently. *Please don't be done with me. I don't want that.* But she couldn't say it out loud.

"Tracy, you have to tell me. I can't read your mind, and when I try to, I fuck it all up. You have to tell me what you want just like I have to tell you. If we don't talk, this won't work. I'll make it easy on you. I'll start."

Slipping down onto one knee, he took both her hands and held them tightly. "Tracy, I love you. I want you. I want it all. I want you to marry me. I want to have children with you. I want us to be forever. Do you want that too?" He kissed both her hands before leaning back on his knee, giving her a little space.

Tracy was shocked. She never expected Dillon to propose. Was this something she was ready for? How did she tell him she needed time, that she wasn't ready yet?

"Oh, Dillon, I...I need some time. It's all happening too soon. I need some space." She pulled herself away from him and stood up, walking into the kitchen, where she had put his keys last night. She took them to him. "I'd like you to go now. I'll call you soon." She handed him his keys and walked to the door, opening it and holding it for him.

Here she was, alone in her house, crying again. Why did she keep doing this?

Dillon sat in his truck for a few minutes before driving home. He thought about going to the club again, but that hadn't worked out so well last night, and didn't think it would be much better now. Maybe Tracy was right, and they both needed some space and time to think, but he knew in his heart that no matter how much time and space she needed, he wasn't going to change his mind, and she would marry him, eventually. Now he just had to convince her of that.

Not wanting to go home, he drove out to Link's. Maybe he could talk Link into shooting some paper at the target range with him. Nothing made him feel better than killing some paper.

Chapter Twelve

Now that Dennis was gone, there was no reason for Tracy to hide anymore. She could go home and see her mother. She had really missed her family and knew they had been hurt by what had happened. She needed to go home and explain. That's what she would do. Her mind made up, she called Dottie to see if they would watch Tickles while she was gone and packed a bag, booking the next flight out on her laptop.

Everything in place, she drove to Derek's and Dottie's to leave her car and the cat. Derek agreed to take her to the airport and pick her up when she got back. He wasn't happy that she hadn't asked Dillon but felt he shouldn't interfere anymore.

Tracy spent several days with her family explaining what had happened and why she had been hiding and unable to contact them. Five years was a long time, and there was a lot of hurt that needed to heal, even though they understood why she needed to do what she had done.

While she was home, she hooked up with several old friends, including Lucy Layton, a girl she had gone to school with. Lucy's husband had left her several months ago, and Lucy was struggling. Tracy suggested she come and stay with her.

Tracy did a lot of thinking while she was home, and one of the decisions she made was to keep the name Tracy. "Mom, I know I will always be your Carrie, but I don't want to go back to being the person Dennis made me. I like who I am now, and hearing that name will just remind me of all he put me through," she explained.

She didn't tell her family about Dillon, but with a mother's intuition, her mother knew. "Honey, I know you're conflicted about this man, but you need to listen to your heart. It will make the best decision for you. Just don't be too hasty. Make him work for you. You're worth it," Tracy's mother told her, hugging her.

Tracy's mom understood, and when it was time to go, they had a tearful goodbye, with Tracy promising to visit more and her mother promising to come and see her now that she could tell them where she was staying.

Tracy enjoyed her time with her parents but was ready to go back to Dillon. She was ready to answer his question now. She knew what she wanted. She just hoped he still wanted the same things she did. She'd only talked to him a few times while she was gone and then not for very long.

It was hard, but the few times Dillon talked with Tracy, he didn't pressure her for an answer or to come home. It was all he could do to keep from picking her up at the airport, but he'd promised her space, and he was going to give her what she needed. He'd been doing some thinking of his own while she was gone and had made some decisions. He was quitting the Secret Service. He was tired of being away so much, and if he and Tracy were going to start a family, he needed to be there for them. Money wasn't a problem, and he didn't need to work. He could help out at the Mix if he got bored. Tyler had been talking about starting an investigative agency, and that sounded interesting. Something they could do from home and manage with a small staff. Now Tracy needed to say yes. If she said no, he didn't know what he was going to do.

Tracy flew in on a Thursday. The next night, Friday, she had a surprise planned for Dillon.

Making a few calls after she got home, she made sure Dillon would be at the club, then took Lucy shopping. She needed some new club wear. This was going to be a very special evening.

Lucy had never been to a club like the Mix and didn't know what to expect. When Tracy had taken her to the fetish shop to buy clothes, she couldn't believe what she'd be wearing, in public, but Tracy assured her that she would fit in perfectly.

Before they left the house, Tracy made sure she could work the security and gave her a set of keys. With a giggle in her voice, Tracy told her, "I don't think I'll be home all weekend."

Tracy planned on meeting Dottie and Tammy at the club. She could leave Lucy with them and not have to worry about abandoning her. She was a little anxious to see Dillon and wondered what he would do to her for leaving like she did. The thought of the things he might do to her would have had her panties damp, if she'd been wearing any, that was.

Tracy led the group of women into the club, feeling confident and ready for what was to come. Tonight she would tell Dillon her answer to his question. A new chapter in her life was about to start, and she was very excited about it.

She had carefully spent the afternoon picking out her outfit, a camisole almost the color of her skin and a very, very short microskirt in black leather. The skirt was so short it barely covered her ass cheeks, and she didn't dare bend over. Seeing Dillon's face as she walked made it all worth the effort. She had spoken with Derek and made sure he was going to be at the club tonight. She had also made sure they had a suite for the weekend. She planned on coming out only for food, and that was all.

When Dillon saw Tracy walk into the club, his jaw almost hit the floor. She looked vibrant and full of confidence and had the biggest smile on her face when she saw him.

How she ran to him in those six-inch heels, he had no idea, but he thoroughly enjoyed it when she launched herself at him and wrapped those mile-long legs around his waist. Gripping her ass under the short skirt, he took her mouth in a kiss that could only be called claiming.

"God, I've missed you, baby," he said.

Looking up into his eyes, Tracy ran her hands through his hair and said, "I've missed you too, and I have the answer you're looking for." Her voice was soft and husky.

Taking a deep breath, she leaned as close as she could get and whispered in his ear, "Yes."

Dillon turned and lifted her so that she was sitting on the bar, and fitted himself between her legs. Stepping back a half step, he looked deep into her eyes. "Yes," he said quietly. "Yes, you'll be mine, marry me, and have my children?"

"If that's what you still want, then yes, I want that too."

Dillon let out a whoop so loud, Tracy almost fell off the bar. Pulling her into his arms, he held her so tight she thought he was going to crush her.

All of their friends crowded around them, slapping Dillon on the back and hugging Tracy, congratulating the couple. Derek brought out bottles of champagne for everyone, and they all celebrated.

After partying with their friends for a while, Tracy led Dillon off to the suite she had reserved. Time for a private celebration.

Pulling Dillon into the room behind her, Tracy closed the door and turned to him. Dropping to her knees, she assumed the position, legs spread, hands palm up on her thighs, and head down. "Master," she said softly, "I'm sorry I left without telling you. I needed some time to come to my senses."

Dillon reached down and pulled her to her feet, lifting her into his arms. Walking over to the bed with her, he dropped her on it and followed her down. Lying on top of her, he grabbed both her arms, pulling them over her head.

"You're mine, and I don't want you to forget that ever. And if you ever pull another trick like that, I'll blister your ass so red, you won't sit for a week," he told her, taking her mouth with passion and need.

Using one hand, he slipped it under her chemise, lifting the silky shirt over her head. Releasing her arms long enough to pull the blouse off, he leaned and took a breast in his mouth, licking, sucking, and nibbling the nipple.

He raised his head long enough to say, "I've missed this and you, baby," before continuing to the other breast.

Sliding one hand down her body, he lifted her skirt to her waist and cupped her mound. Lifting himself off of her, he pulled her skirt and shoes off and stepped to the side of the bed to remove his clothes. Standing there naked, he looked at her.

"No more condoms?" he asked. Now that she had said yes, he wanted to start their family as soon as possible.

Tracy smiled and nodded, the thought of little Dillons running around in her head. She saw how happy Dottie and Derek were with Micah, and now they were expecting their second child. Tyler and Tammy were pregnant too, and there would be lots of children for her child to grow up and play with.

She was excited to start a family, kids, a home, the life she'd always wanted. Without the threat of Dennis looming over her head, she was free to enjoy life and have fun.

Dillon looked down at his woman. He couldn't wait to be able to call her his wife, see her belly stretched with his child. His life was changing for the better.

While she had been visiting her family, Derek had turned him on to a property for sale not far from his and Tyler's places. He couldn't wait to show it to her. He wanted to sit with her and plan their house, where they would live and raise their family.

Now it was time to start working on that family. Laying himself on the bed beside her, he cupped her face with his hand before kissing her again and lifting himself over her. Holding himself above her, he leaned down so that his lips were almost touching hers and said, "Don't think you got out of your punishment, but right now, I can't wait any longer." Fitting his cock to her opening, he filled her with one thrust, going so deep his balls hit her ass.

Tracy screamed and dug her nails into his back. This was what she'd been missing. Wrapping her legs around so that her heels were in his ass, she held him and pulled him closer, if that were possible.

Dillon thrust himself in and out, holding his release back as long as possible. Taking one nipple between his teeth, he pulled, and slipped one hand between their bodies, rubbing her clit until she was as ready as he was. Giving her that final pinch to set her off, he followed her climax with his own, capturing the scream she made with his mouth. He never wanted to leave her.

Tracy threaded her hands in Dillon's hair and pulled his head closer, holding him to her. She was never letting him go.

Dillon collapsed on Tracy, lying on her softness for a minute before rolling to one side and pulling her close. "Rest, baby. Then we'll play."

They spent the weekend in the suite, surfacing only for food and briefly going into the club Saturday for another quick celebration with their friends. Tracy felt a little guilty for leaving Lucy but knew Dottie and Tammy would watch over her.

Chapter Thirteen

Since Tracy didn't care about a big wedding, it took very little planning for the small gathering they had. Tracy's parents were there, of course, and all of their friends. Lucy stood up with Tracy and Derek with Dillon. They were married in Derek's backyard six weeks after Tracy said yes.

Two days after the wedding, Tammy had her baby, a girl they named Erica.

Two months later, Dottie had her little girl, Julia. By then Tracy was three months pregnant with her own child.

She and Dillon bought the property he had been looking at and designed their own house with a little help. Doing most of the work themselves, they really felt the house was theirs. Tracy quit her job but stayed available on a consulting basis, helping with the investigative agency Tyler was establishing.

Her life was perfect now. She had Dillon, she had friends, she was back in contact with her family, and soon she would have one of her own. She had all the happiness she had ever dreamed of.

THE END

Don't miss out!

Visit the website below and you can sign up to receive emails whenever Rose Nickol publishes a new book. There's no charge and no obligation.

https://books2read.com/r/B-A-QFBG-GNEQB

BOOKS2READ

Connecting independent readers to independent writers.

Also by Rose Nickol

All the President's Men
Derek's Darling Damsel
Dillion's Dainty Delight

Ashcroft Security
Ashcroft Security Saving Lena

Club de Fleur
Club de Fleurs 3: Theresa`
Club de Fleurs 4: Rachel
Club de Fleurs 5: Tina's Twins
Club de Fleurs 2 Sadie
Club de Fleurs Tasha
Club de Fleur Melissa

Club de Fleurs
Club de Fleurs: Jenna

Daddies' Lost Girls
Litte Girl Lost

Heroes of the Heart
Rescuing Their Love Hereos of the Heart Book One
Rescuing Their Love Heroes of the Heart Book Two

Kodiak Matings
Bearly Mated

Standalone
Kodiak Matings Bearly Mated

Watch for more at rosenickol.com.